Rick Weeks

BOXED UP!

A group of misfits - thrown together on a crippled
container ship.

Chapter 1. A&E

The day had started badly for him with an argument at the traffic lights. On reflection he was unwise to sound the car horn quite so quickly at the scaffolding lorry in front. The three second delay caused by the momentary traffic pause was insignificant next to the additional three painful hours spent in A&E. As the bemused Junior Doctor, freshly qualified from the Accra Redemption Clinic explained, baseball bats can't be removed painlessly but once washed down with hot soapy water they're as good as new.

Back in his cubicle at the Planning Office, a barked lesson about the morality of lateness by his cruel but fair boss Len Lies compounded the feeling of gloom. Where was the outspoken maverick of earlier years? So many ideas..Now he'd been re-incarnated as *The Cubicle Mouse: Crag Slate*.

Was it really too late to change? He set his lantern jaw at the leaden clouds outside his window and looked quizzically through narrowed steely blue eyes at the darkening afternoon gloom as the never ending stream of cars navigated the soulless roundabout.

Being a person of incredible personal vanity, he found it difficult to resist the temptation to look at his reflection in the plate glass. He admired his coiffured hair, set in a style somewhere between a 50's Teddy Boy and James Bond.It had an almost acrylic sheen, but his crowning glory was the luxuriant, recently clipped moustache, closely modelled on Magnum PI. He tried to settle into his work, acutely aware of the discomfort of sitting down, little realising how his life was about to be changed forever..

Chapter 2. Clams

Later that evening he met the woman he worshiped from afar as he took the evening air past the ruined gun emplacements.

'Hello' purred Esmee breathily.'I've just had two large glasses of the world's finest absinthe and am feeling all unnecessary. What shall I do Crag, you're a good man with a cliche. The fate of my modesty might be in your hands.'

'You're right' barked Crag snapping shut his inhaler. 'But two glasses is not enough. I once needed three glasses of the intoxicating liquid to save the east-side quadrant. I must tell you about that one day'. He grinned clenching his pipe. By now Esmee was swooning." Let's go down to the waters edge" she gasped," I've heard tell there be indigenous Land Clams romping over the Greensward." They walked along the beach carefully avoiding the clams and their long proboxces. As she studied his finely chiseled moustache and his over-styled hair she felt a strange weakness in her legs.
They walked along, each consumed in their own silence. Bizarrely he found himself thinking about the old Carry-On films. "Do you like eating clams?" she offered. "Oooh Maatronn !! " he riposted, feeling strangely cool and spontaneous. She tried to cover her embarrassment by singing a selection of the more humorous verses from the North Korean National Anthem. As he turned up his collar at the impending rain, he stopped and stooped, grim-faced, to pick up a dog-eared photo washed up by the tide…

Chapter 3. Drinks

Heavy raindrops spattered the old photo. He studied the picture intently, his piecing blue eye framed by his freshly adjusted
weather beaten monocle. His mind raced back to earlier days when the monocle had been new. His father had given it to him on his second birthday as an aid to his disguise.

'Why!' exclaimed Esmee, I do believe I recognise that man. I'm sure he's one of the legendary Monks who fled from the ruined Thought Monastery on that ill fated night'..'Stop' he commanded masterfully. 'We don't mention that night around these parts. Let's get out of this rain and head for that gloomy solitary pub on the cliff-top'.
The pub was quiet with just a quartet of fishermen singing selections from the Nuremberg rallies. Crag drew deeply on his rough cask bitter through a carved ivory straw while Esmee toyed with her cocktail.'We don't get much call for them cocktails round these parts' the landlord quipped before Crag fixed him with a stare of pure disgust.'Back to your harmonium landlord! Play us a tune and make it snappy'. The harmonium slowly wheezed back into life and the fishermen resumed their collective foreign reprises.

He felt tired as he re-loaded his pipe with its unique blend of rough hewn shag obtained for him by a trusted lackey just off the Burlington Arcade.He tried to concentrate on the picture through the smokey, purple haze. Esmee had finished her cocktail and was vigorously dancing the Polka with each of the clientele in turn, throwing her head back and laughing insanely. The room was spinning faster and faster. Crag grasped on to the table top to stop himself falling and concentrated on the picture.The face seemed to be laughing back at him, mocking his memory. He had to get outside for air.The music was growing louder. Esmee was dancing, faster and faster.She had become a spinning, exciting blur...he felt himself being pulled down into the void and then engulfed and then silence…

Chapter 4. At Sea

His head felt swollen. His skull was trying to burst as he became aware of the flicker and buzz of grubby fluorescent lights hurting his head. Groggily Crag clasped his strong manly tanned hand to his throbbing forehead. 'Where am I?' he gasped..He began to take in the nauseous smell of exhaust and old engine oils mixed with the dull, regular thudding of machinery.
'You're somewhere safe' she murmured.'Somewhere where nothing can harm you. We're on a container ship, heading down the Channel, can't you hear the engines? We had to get out of the country fast. We're on a slow boat to China to be rendered and recycled. Don't worry. Before we end up as premium protein cake(PPC),there are places this ship stops at en-route. So we get the choices of some great cities to investigate and have a good time, yay!'
'I say but !' stuttered Crag. 'What about the mission I'm actively involved with? Do I just throw it all away? Do I just forget about the fight between good and evil and discard my lantern-jaw? What about my moustache?'.
He reached down to adjust his trousers into a more appropriate stance. She glanced down in appreciation.
Esmee's mind returned to that crazy, abandoned night she spent dancing the Polka. She half-remembered those urgent, lit, eager faces. She put the photo in her mouth and chewed thoughtfully.
'Stop!' he cried, too late as she swallowed…

Chapter 5. Etiquette

After a few days at sea, the mistaken consumption of the photo was forgotten.Esmee had been most profuse in her apologies and Crag was in a mellow state of mind pondering what to wear for the evening. They had received an embossed request for their presence tonight for dinner at the Captain's Table. Crag opted for his favourite white safari suit with the lightweight pith. Esmee, aware of a nautical theme, went for the semi-sheer jersey garnished with limpets.

They were surprised when the steward showed them to a small, modest table barely a yard across, topped by formica with a scratched and faded blue gingham print.'Here we are.. may I present the Captains Table!' gushed the steward,'he's owned this since his childhood, a present from Keith Moon'.

'Where's the Captain' barked an exacerbated Crag,'we have an embossed Invitation'.

'Ahh yes ahem..some slight technical problems. The captain is detained in the engine room.' The steward was busy blustering. 'We lost all power three hours ago.I'm afraid we're drifting sir'

'Stand Back !'roared Crag 'I'll soon have this old tub back slicing through the briny!'.

Esmee gasped in admiration. She felt the need to sit down and cool off.When she came round she saw him disappear below decks and into the engine room.

The vessel they were on, the Lagos Star had an unhappy history. Originally she was built as a car ferry but the loss of her two sister ships in mysterious circumstances had shaken investor confidence. She had been hastily converted to take scrap cars to Africa for their second-hand car market. Unfortunately an accident during loading with a fork-lift had resulted in a fire which had significantly weakened the ship's structure, leaving the vessel unsafe and without official permission to put to sea. A Serbian P.O.Box company had superficial repairs carried out by a Somali shipyard and the ship was relaunched with a new certificate as a medcap container vessel.

Meanwhile below decks

Chapter 6. Control

The smell of burning oil mixed with the acrid remnants of electrics met with Crag as he stumbled into the engine room where the Captain crouched snivelling in between the two defunct engines."I'm not a real captain" he sobbed,"I was left behind when the other Somali pirates left. I thought they were my friends but they play cruel joke on me, saying I was an old, how you say 'slowliabilitycoach' and so they leave me behind". Crag knew he would have to pull on his deepest reserves learnt from his Safety in the Workplace courses to marshal this gibbering fool to perform."Good God man!" he barked."Pull yourself together! Think of your tented family on the beach.Do you want to be remembered as a washed-up wannabe or a proud pirate?"
The Captain slowly rose from his knees, pulling up his trousers.He drew himself to full height."I haff un plan" he sneered confidently as his accent changed.
" Quick, up to ze bridge!"

The Captain had a twin half-brother born in Bremmen who had successfully commanded U-Boat U57 through many war time conflicts and was highly decorated.(him not the boat)

On the bridge they soon found the problem. The ships' Central Navigational and Engineering computer had been disconnected. It had been unplugged to make way for a microwave cooker that was still warm with the pungent whiff of biryani.
Crag removed his monocle, polished it on his safari lapels and replaced it close to his eyeball. He cradled his lantern jaw in his large tanned hand.He smoothed down his disturbed over-styled hair. He pinched the crease in his trousers and adjusted his fly. Finally he lightly trimmed his moustache.
Images of betrayal were crowding into his analytical mind
"The Steward" he growled, "can we trust that steward?"..

Chapter 7. Cards

The issue of the Steward's and Captain's loyalty was in no doubt as they were seen the next day jumping overboard, screaming " We're all going to die!"

Crag and Esmee stumbled dazed and confused through the drifting, abandoned ship.The silence was complete, broken only by the wind and occasional creaking protest of a swinging bulkhead door, losing its battle against rust.

While Crag dismantled the microwave using primitive cave tools, Esmee investigated some of the containers stacked on deck. As she walked through one of the narrow alleys between the weathered steel, her ears sharpened as she thought she heard the call of a bird.

She followed the sound, a deep squawk, to a container at the end of the row, and tried the handle.

She was met with a rush of exotic after-shave and the smell of fine tobacco.Sitting by a green baize covered card table, back-lit by an ornate red standard lamp sat Omah Sharif.

"I suppose you heard the Griffon" he announced, fixing Esmee with night-dark smouldering eyes. "She helps me to concentrate on the cards. Do you play?"

So many questions were racing through Esmee's head. What was Omah Sharif doing on a rust bucket container ship? Why did he choose to live in a container? Why did he have a pet Griffon? What was that after-shave?

"I expect you're wondering why I live on a container ship?" he enquired stroking his moustache and spreading out a pack of cards."Here I have no distractions. It helps me to concentrate on the cards.How about a rubber?"

Esmee flushed and stared into his eyes "a rubber..oh yes please!" she trilled without thinking.She was mesmerised by his dark eyes and stupendous moustache, full and flowing. She imagined it brushing against her smooth white skin. So different from Crag's mean and clipped excuse for facial hair.

"Come over to the sofa and I will show you a few of my tricks" he murmured, picking up some cards from the table. Esmee moved hesitantly across the floor to join him on the under-stuffed sofa. She tried to pull down the short hem of her thin dress. She realised she was still wearing the semi-sheer jersey from last night but the limpets had now fallen off, showing more of her than she would have liked.

"Have you seen how I can balance cards on a woman's breast?" he whispered.

"Why don't you show me?" she invited.

He slipped the dress off her shoulders. "Lay down and I will build the Taj Mahal of cards on your body, complete in every detail it will be my life's work!" He was becoming over animated. His eyes were now wild and staring." I can arrange for deliveries of more cards and some food for you. Every day I will build more of this glorious Temple to Womanhood. Of course you will have to lie there every day but I bring in some magazines so you don't get bored".

Esmee was having very serious misgivings about Mr Sharif and his plan when the Griffon squawked a warning and the door flew open…

Chapter 8. Feathers

"You foreign swine!! Unhand that woman immediately !" roared Crag as Esmee struggled to her feet clutching the flimsy dress to her breasts. Playing cards which had been destined for body art, lay scattered across the floor's multi-coloured, swirling excuse for a carpet.

"Let's not have any trouble old man" mocked Omah cradling his favourite Luger pistol."Oh yes.. this" he laughed, waving the gun around. "The Captain's twin half-brother lost it to me at cards".

Crag was stunned into silence. The Griffon had settled on his shoulder and was annoyingly pecking at his over-styled hair."You mean the Captain's German twin half-brother is here ? On this ship?"

"Sure" smiled Omah," he lives one box up three along. Real nice inside, just like a Bavarian lodge. Five along the same level is the Old Bent Crone. She don't get out much."

Crag stroked his manly over-sized jaw and toyed with his weak moustache, his over-styled hair glinting like steel in the low light from the table. He had remembered something.

Omah started shuffling some cards and leered at Esmee."Now baby,what about that Taj Mahal?"

At that point the giant griffon unexpectedly swooped, snatching the cards off a shocked Omah.

"Looks like the rubber's off, Omah" chortled Esmee with withering scorn as the bird ran amok in the confined space.

Yet all was not yet lost. Not for nothing had Esmee led the hockey team to it's pinnacle of glory. Raising her finely muscled forearm she caught the bird a stinging blow on it's cruppers. "Take that" she fluted as the big bird collapsed.

Crag watched in hushed admiration... "I say" he nervously gulped.

"Time for tea I think" announced Esmee...

[Recap: Lantern jawed buffoon Crag Slate,together with fey,impressionable Esmee have found themselves trapped on a disabled container ship with no crew but a mysterious group of characters and shadowy recluses. What dark unspoken secret links these unlikely characters? The unfathomable mystery continues...]

Chapter 9. Tea

They left Omah to clean up his container.

"I've never seen cruppers explode like that" marvelled Crag as they picked their way along a rusted gangway with Esmee swinging the collected grisly parts in a bin bag."Will the bird be OK?".

"Oh yes" laughed Esmee, "they keep growing back and get bigger every time."

They found a spare container and made themselves at home. Esmee busied herself with a kettle."Earl Grey or Cruppers?" she breathed "Any Baron Black?" he growled."I'll have to check" she murmured suggestively as she polished her cups.

"Would you care for the silver or a nice bone china?" she inquired.

"Have you a nice DD?" he asked roguishly. Fortunately she was raised in a convent so did not understand and continued demurely placing the grisly parts in a teapot.

"Hmm.. nice pair of jugs" he persisted, gazing at her shelves. "This cruppers tea has a strange but interesting aftertaste.."

"It's the terroir" she chortled downing her steaming cup in seconds.

"Did you know I have a sister?" she enquired over the steam.

Crag sprayed his tea over the floor, splashing his safari trousers with a dark stain. He looked down in embarrassment. Esmee quickly looked away.

"You never told me" he spluttered "where is she?"

"I don't know" she retorted, "she was a cleaner working in Switzerland, on the Hadron Collider. One day there was an accident.They were doing stress tests while she was busy polishing the collider.They forgot she was inside. When the tests were finished she had disapeared. The report said she had been transported as anti-matter. A bit like Star-Trek they said. They didn't know where. She could be anywhere."

Crag was surreptitiously examining the wet patch on his trousers wondering how it could be removed without domestic help. "Damn that Steward" he thought,"tossing himself off over the side like that."

"Oh drinks..wonderful!" trilled Esmee. Crag spun round, clenching his pipe, just in time to see a soaked figure in the doorway holding a drinks tray....

Chapter 10. Liquid

Crag stared in disbelief at the dripping apparition of a drenched and seaweed covered Steward standing in the doorway. He was holding a drinks tray containing a bottle of Cahtspiece single-malt and two glasses."Ahem..I do apologise for the interruption sir but was thinking you might be needing some refreshment."

"Ooh.. you're back," trilled Esmee "how nice!"

"Good God man!" barked Crag,"the last time I saw you,you were floating off with the Captain. Where is he ?"

"Ahem.."explained the Steward,"I'm afraid the sea-water did not agree with him sir, and his body simply dissolved."

"Dissolved you say?" Crag adjusted his trousers in disbelief and glanced again at his embarrassing wet patch."Oh well, while you're here, can you do anything with this stain?"

"Of course sir, straight away.Oh..and sir.It is my understanding that there will be a drinks party tonight at the Captain's German half-brothers abode and all are welcome.

"Yay!" a party wooped Esmee,"what fun, what shall I wear?".

Crag had been hoping to spend a quiet night attending to his wardrobe and physical appearance but reluctantly agreed."Well, What's the Captains German half-brother's name Steward?" he asked guardedly.

"I believe it's Sven sir," said the Steward looking fixedly into Crag's eyes...

Chapter 11. Party

There was an air of visceral excitement as they prepared for the evening's drinks party.Esmee had made some running repairs to her flimsy, semi-sheer mini-dress and had increased it's allure with the addition of gift tokens. Crag had struggled with his choice of evening wear. Both the cream and the pale blue Safari suits had seemed inappropriate and the white suit was out of action due to an embarrassing stain. Finally after much deliberation he decided on his one piece turquoise mankini with the extra large gusset.He felt this would give the necessary air of gravitas while reducing the risk of unexpected protrusions. A full-length black moleskin cape completed the ensemble. A final trim of his moustache and he was ready.

As they opened the steel door to Sven's container (*the Captain's German twin half-brother, highly decorated ex U -Boat commander),* the noise hit them. There was a large group of people, laughing loudly, clinking glasses and drinking. A smooth pianist was tinkling on a baby grand in the corner. The air was heavy with tobacco smoke and perfume.

Omah Sharif sidled up to them."Ah the delightful Esmee with her buffoon protector" he laughed,"I didn't realise tonight was fancy-dress!" Crag's moustache bristled."Now look here.."he began. "Cool it Robin, just a joke,"replied Omah as his hungry eyes started to slide down Esmee's gift tokens. She tugged at the hem nervously, feeling her knees shake.

Crag looked around the room and suddenly felt out of his depth. There were people there he thought he'd 'd seen on TV. Famous, confident faces looked back at him. He recognised a recently disgraced Politician puffing on a cigar. There was an ageing rock star wanted by the authorities, an Old Bent Crone, and a powerful Anglo-Swedish industrialist with long fingernails who reminded Crag of Howard Hughes.

Amongst this glittering ensemble the Steward moved effortlessly. He weaved through the throng with ease, dispensing drinks with an uncanny accuracy, perfectly remembering every individual's preference.

The Steward was in his element. Everyone was having a lovely time and it was his Stewardship that was making it all happen.

Crag's gimlet gaze noticed a man sitting on his own in the corner. "Who's that?" demanded Crag to the Steward, roughly grabbing his arm, spilling the tray of drinks. "Ahem..that's our host sir, that's Sven."

Crag's eyes went back to the man and then back to Crag. Crag was hypnotised by the seated figure before him. He seemed somehow familiar but how could he tell? It wasn't just the robe and hookah that confounded him. Whereas a hookah pipe would normally have been held by two lips, here it disappeared into a small bandaged slit.

Apart from the two dark slits for the eyes, there was a tight, white, plaster bandage completely enclosing the man's face, head and neck....

Chapter 12. Jealousy

Crag felt like tapping the plastered head and asking if anyone was at home.The wispy smoke issuing from the slit seemed to indicate that there was. So many questions that needed answers. Unfortunately he was distracted as he noticed a particularly flattering pose of himself in a nearby mirror.

He looked over at Omah, who was showing off, waving his pistol around, being loud and drunk "Hey Robin, come over here and get your ass whipped !" he shouted, much to everyone's delight."Let's see how much of a man you really are!"

Crag was rapidly going off Omah. He disliked his casual, laid-back approach, his cool confidence. He hated the way he undressed Esmee with his eyes but most of all he hated the fact that Omah's dark and flowing moustache was far superior to his own.

"Oh, very funny Omah!" lied Crag,"have you a licence for that thing?"

"Which one," laughed Omah as he reached down into his fly and produced his impressive member."This one?"

The party roared with laughter at Omah's antics. Crag was beginning to wish he'd spent the evening attending to his toilet as he felt the mankini gussett tighten.

Suddenly there was a scream from Esmee. "Eeek!.. Sis!..Sis darling is it really you?" Crag spun round from the mirror to see Esmee clutching a woman of Amazonian proportions.She was covering the woman in kisses and holding her tightly in a childlike hug. "Everybody! Listen!" she announced,"this is my sister. I've found her again after all these years.This is the happiest day of my life!"

Crag was confused. He re-loaded his pipe with the unique blend of rough shag from his trusted lackey off the Burlington Arcade and let his mind wander as the smoke started to play tricks with his brain. The party and the noise started receding into an impressionistic tableau of blurred indistinct figures. He looked across at the bandaged Sven, seated upright and motionless in the corner and felt himself drifting away....

Chapter 13. Hair

"Last night," he blurted groggily, did all that really happen?"
"Ooh yes" smirked Esmee," it really did for me.I had a simply divine time."
Crag's mind was blank. He remembered an audience of strangely weaving figures just before he had passed out. "You silly boy," admonished Esmee,"we were only there for ten minutes before you passed out. Some of Omah's tricks were breathtaking and that Sven is an absolute scream." Crag sullenly ironed his trousers in silence measuring the creases with a slide-rule. His chances to investigate further had been thwarted. He had foolishly been duped. Who were these people and why were they all thrust together on this drifting hulk? He had missed a golden chance find out. He tried not to show his remorse.
"That Omah's certainly good with cards" he proffered. "Oh no, he's a lot more than that." said Esmee knowingly, "anyway my Sis has invited us both round to her place later today. Apparently she's gone for the Borneo jungle look, can't wait to see it."
Crag was apprehensive.He looked askance at Esmee and wondered how was she able to absorb the events that were happening to them in that delightful, throw away manner. She flitted through life like a tropical butterfly.
Crag rapidly bought himself to his senses, had a cold shower and began to plan his jungle ensemble. Obviously the lightweight pith was essential, together with the white safari and the freshly laundered trousers.He was toying in the mirror with an amusing cravat when he noticed he would have to spend some manicure time on his ear- hair which due to a lack of recent attention had begun to de-stabilise his elaborate coiffure.
As they stepped out in the afternoon sun,Crag looked resplendent in his safari whites, while Esmee wore an oriental robe which looked remarkably like Sven's. They made their way along the steel walkway to Sis's container...

Chapter 14. Jungle

As Crag put his hand on the door to Sis's container he could feel the heat emanating from the steel. Swinging the door open, the warm sticky heat enveloped them like a blanket, closing around them. Crag tilted his lantern-jaw up at the steaming canopy wondering how he had found himself in this dangerous garden of survival where something malicious lurked behind every leaf. How he yearned for the safety of his cubicle at the Planning Office where he would now be, quietly tutting over the latest interruption to his tea break.

"Tea ?" a voice asked as if from nowhere.Crag's gimlet eyes scanned the dripping foliage and saw Esmee's sister sitting cross-legged at a small teapot and stove.She was wearing a chamois leather loincloth with matching halter, a string of native beads and nothing else. "I've had to improvise and make it from gathered shoots and leaves, but there's still some good strong cruppers in it,"she said.
"As long as there's cruppers in it, that's good enough for me," he quipped, flicking off a leech. He marvelled at the tea making abilities of these two sisters.
He looked at the two girls, sisters but so very different. Esmee, fey, white skinned, petit and blond, her sister, strong, brown with brawny muscular arms and carrying some splendid tattoos.
Crag found himself drawn to Sis's body art. The tattoos spread down from her neck and arms to below her waist.They mostly featured nautical or Goth themes, depicting some splendid mythical creatures but the piece de resistance was a recent addition showing a magnificent Lord of the Rings tableau.
"I say..!" slurped Crag as Sis started showing him the tattooist's work.
"Do you like it?" she offered, turning to show him her back.
"I..I've never seen a snake do that before," he quipped tastelessly as she bent over to pour the tea…

Chapter 15. Doldrums

The days passed by slowly on board the stricken *Lagos Star*.
An air of routine had settled on Esmee as she spent her days wandering along the decks and walkways talking to whoever was about. Often when the weather was foul she would be on her own, holding onto the ships rail, looking out to sea. Sometimes, if they drifted near a shipping lane, she would see another container ship ploughing past, too busy to stop where time and money were involved. It would be heading East with a full load for recycling. An ironic role reversal from the ancient tea-clippers that used to race West from the Orient with their exotic, expensive cargos. When the weather was fair she would try and seek out company amongst the strange group of recluses, making conversation when it allowed. One hot, still,day when the sea was mirror flat and the sky an unbroken blue, she happened upon the Old Bent Crone sitting outside her container. She was seated on an old wickerwork straight backed rocking chair ,dressed in black, mumbling quiet incantations whilst letting the worn beads of a rosary slip through her gnarled fingers. She stared hard as Esmee approached. "Helloo," trilled Esmee,"it's so lovely to meet you, can I join you?"
"My first is in Leviticus but not in Duplication," mumbled the Crone,"what do you want from me?"
"It's such a lovely day, I thought perhaps we could talk," gushed Esmee in a friendly non-hostile opening gambit."I'm from England, Gloomworth actually, on the North-East coast, near the old Abbey."
The Old Bent Crone's worn, weatherbeaten face turned the colour of alabaster as the blood drained away."Leave me alone! Why won't you people leave me alone!" she cried, getting to her feet and slamming the door behind her leaving the wickerwork chair silently rocking.
"Oh dear" mused Esmee," not a good start."
Meanwhile Crag was below decks in the engine room trying to revive the defunct engines. He had spent the last few weeks attempting to rewire the microwave using string but had to admit defeat when a nasty explosion had almost destroyed the bridge, together with the creases in his pale-blue safari trousers. He now turned his attention to examining the giant twin diesel engines where he could smell the unmistakable odour of leaking fuel…

Chapter 16. Hands-on

In the gloom of the engine room Crag got to work. He furrowed his broad brow and concentrated on the job in-hand.He had a limited selection of tools at his disposal but was determined to show he was the man for Esmee. He was annoyed by the intrusion of Omah who seemed to have snarled her in his web of carefree fun.

"Fun," he muttered to himself,"Fun...I'll show that greasy foreigner. I'll save this old tub and get us all to safety. I'll be a hero and she'll swoon into my arms."

He looked around him at the bubbling batteries giving off highly-inflammable gases and the ever increasing pool of fuel collecting on the engine room floor.

He opened his toolbox and selected a primitive cave tool. He worked feverishly as beads of sweat trickled down his face, chiseled into concentration. He was imagining himself portrayed as a crack bomb-disposal expert. Lives depended on the right wire to connect.

He used string and card to bypass and short-circuit the electrical controls. His hand carved ivory drinking straw was used to good effect as a fuel bridge and an emergency flare gun was pressed into service as a starter.

He sat back and admired his work. He felt strong and confident. That old rusted propeller would soon be turning again. Time for a manly pipe of rough shag. He reached for his tobacco.

The explosion, a deep, bellowing roar, blasting it's way up for air from below decks, could be heard everywhere on the ship.

At the bow, people were on deck, listening to an impromptu concert by the ageing rock-star who was just segueing into another mind-changing guitar solo of glorious cerebral masturbation. The audience was cheering him on. He'd already demolished two Marshall stacks and was working on number three when the deck lurched sickeningly sideways.The audience roared him on with encouragement as the volume went up to number eleven.

Everywhere else, people had heard and felt the explosion and were gathering, confused in a group on deck. "Where's Crag?" someone asked. The ship, on cue, lurched further sideways.

Esmee looked around nervously and swallowed hard…

Chapter 17. Humiliation

There was screaming panic as the decks started tilting and objects started sliding towards the rail. Then people seemed to freeze in mid-step, as, with an agonising slowness, the deadly list slowly corrected itself and the old creaking ship gradually hauled herself back upright one more time.
"Time for a drink," drawled Omah, without a hair out of place.
As they stared into the smoke drifting from the blown open cargo hatch, they saw two figures. One was a hairless, blackened man with the tattered, burnt remains of a safari suit trailing behind him. The other a smallish dapper figure wearing a Steward's uniform and carrying a tray of drinks.
"Hooray !" shrieked Esmee,"everybody's safe! My hero !" as she rushed over to the Steward and hugged his tightly uniformed body to her trembling, melting limbs.
Crag stood forlornly to one side, his wide, white eyes looking out from an oily, blackened face.
"So what will you do now Mr Mechanic?" sneered Omah, as he perused the barbecued Crag up and down, "a few bars of 'Mammy' perhaps ?"
Someone in the group started giggling and before long they were all laughing uncontrollably, pointing hysterically at Crag and congratulating Omah on the jest.
The ultimate humiliation was complete ..Crag turned and wearily dragged himself back to the container. He had failed again...miserably. He looked at the black, hairless head staring back from the mirror and sobbed…

Chapter 18. Hero

Once it had been ascertained that the ship was not actually sinking, people started returning to their normal routine. Steward took Esmee back to his container for a stiff drink and to provide her with some re-assurance about what had happened.
"So..um you saved Crag's life?" she asked.
"Well..ahem, in a way," deferred the Steward. "I went down to the engine room to enquire if he was in need of some liquid refreshment, when I noticed he was about to light his pipe in what could only be described as the most dangerous of circumstances. Initially he was annoyed with my intrusion muttering about 'interrupting a man's work' but finally we agreed to take the drinks outside where he could enjoy his pipe. Unfortunately as

he stopped to make safe the equipment, he accidentally set the flare-gun timer, which,after some delay, went off just as we vacated the room. I think you know the rest."

Esmee chewed on an old photo carefully and thought about Crag's valiant attempt.

"Will he be alright?" she asked. "Oh, I'm sure he'll be fine in a couple of days,"encouraged the Steward," and his hair will probably grow back eventually."

"Well my heartfelt thanks to you Steward," trilled Esmee,"by the way I don't even know your name, what is it?"

"Stewart madam. Stewart Steward. I come from a long line of Stewards. My grandfather re-arranged the deckchairs on the Titanic."

Esmee felt strangely drawn towards this man. As she sipped her second brandy she found herself sidling along the sofa towards his re-assuring uniform…

Chapter 19. Vanity

Back in the container Crag looked at his reflected mess in the mirror. He'd taken a shower and had been relieved to find most of the oily blackness on his face had finally washed off, leaving a few small cuts and burns, now fetchingly covered by steri-strips.

His hair however was a different matter. His glorious over-styled pompadour had been ruined. Instead of the lush dark waves and pinnacles, coaxed into an elaborate tribute to the hairdressers art, there were left just a few stunted, burnt sprigs from a dead forest fire. His moustache, once a clipped icon of his brusque virility, had all but disappeared leaving a few limp, pathetic strands... He looked ridiculous.

He tried some different poses with his best pal; the mirror. He swung half-right,half-left. He tried thrusting his lantern-jaw at different, rakish angles. All to no avail. He looked like a Russian circus clown, whose Trabant had just blown up.

Hs he sat down heavily, feeling dejected and morose. The door opened and Esmee tripped in lightly humming an amusing ditty. Crag's shrewed eyes perceived she was somewhat disheveled with her messed hair and stained dress but he chose to say nothing.

"Oooh ! Look at you soldier!" she drooled,"let me do something with that silly hair."

Within minutes she had set up some shaving foam and razor and was lathering his face and head "Hmm, first The Black and White Minstrels and now the Marshmallow Man" she laughed.

Crag could say nothing. He had never felt so naked. He sat in silence as Esmee worked skilfully with the razor, removing the ragged tufts of hair from his head and upper-lip.

Finally she had finished. There was nothing she could save. She'd had to carefully shave off moustache, eye-brow and hair remnants, everything had gone.

"Oooh sexy man," she purred as she rubbed aromatic oils into his shaved head, face and neck."Hey presto ! The new you !" as she proffered the mirror.

Crag saw a gaunt, robotic face from a prison colony looking back at him but was more concerned that Esmee would notice the alarming way his trousers had made a perfect facsimile of the North Face of the Eiger. He had never felt so pleasantly excited. He wondered if he could ask Esmee for some more of that oil.

"Umm,a.. any chance of another massage," he croaked.

"Sure why not ," purred Esmee as she deftly unleashed his belt...

Chapter 20. Foiled

She knelt before him, gently applying the oil to her hands, and looked directly up into his eyes. She had a wide-eyed look he hadn't seen before. It wasn't harsh or unpleasant but honest. An honest appraisal of the man she was kneeling before and about to handle intimately.

"I say ! blurted Crag in an embarrassed attempt to say something - anything - to prevent himself falling over the edge into those wonderful warm eyes, where he knew, he could effortlessly dive with her, deep into the universe.

He looked down and was aghast to see an acorn where a vertical masterpiece had just been. "Hell's teeth!" he clenched, "bloody embarrassing, eh-what?"

Esmee wiped her hands clean with a paper towel and smiled kindly at Crag."Don't worry Soldier, you've been through a lot lately..me too."

Crag was wishing he could curl himself up into a tight ball and roll into a dark corner..

"Methinks time for Tea...bounced back Esmee,"I've invited Sis and Sven round. Such fun..!"

Chapter 21. Communication

Sis and Sven arrived laughing. After the initial introductions (Sven,sis,sis sven snevs,sne),they sat around drinking and relaxing. Esmee was busy serving tea and fussing over Sven's hookah. Occasionally she playfully tickled the bandage where she thought his chin was. To communicate, he'd taken to writing words in chalk on a small blackboard whenever he had something he wanted to say. It reminded Esmee of the Bob Dylan song, 'Subterranean Homesick Blues', where Bob holds up cardboard cue cards written in felt-tip as the song moves along.

Crag was suffering a major identity crisis. One minute he was the suave, hirsute hero complete with over-styled hair and macho moustache, the next, a lookalike serial-killer on death row, waiting for the Govenor's call with a flat battery.

"Pull yourself together man" he muttered to himself under his breath,"just because you've undergone an identity transplant, there's a mystery to be solved here and you're the man to do it!"

He felt better after the morale boosting chat with himself and he began to think how he could save the ship. There had to be another way of turning those rusty propellers. His inquisitive mind began to wander to the large store of everyday fertiliser in handy sacks, stored enticingly next to some faulty army detonators en-route to a puppet dictatorship. He was devising a plan.

Esmee was in a joyous mood, frolicking and laughing while Sven showed her some very rude chalk drawings on his board. Some of them were extremely correct anatomically and she was guffawing with very un-lady like belly laughs. Sven's head bandage occasionally twitched, or creased and made a slight movement so he seemed to be having a good time too. Crag had surreptitiously been ogling Sis's tattoos from a distance when she swaggered over to him and made some small-talk."Having a good look are we? So, my sister's not good enough for you eh? Who the hell do you think you are, Mr God's Gift From On High? You pervert - I'd like to slap you around a bit but you'd take it personally and then I'd really have to hurt you."

Crag sighed and reached for his trusty, heavily charred tobacco tin…

Chapter 22. Urine

Crag sat with his pipe clenched between his teeth staring out to sea, drawing little comfort from the rough hewn shag obtained from his little man just off the Burlington Arcade. He pondered how things hadn't really gone as planned and he appeared to be the ship's laughing stock. If it was possible to have a nautical version of the village idiot, he was the main contender for the role. He needed to restore his reputation. He reminded himself how all that would change once he'd saved the ship from disaster. His feverish brain was formulating the Grand Plan.

As he sat watching the greasy, heaving swell he was acutely aware of being enveloped in an exotic aroma. He turned and was surprised to find the bandaged Sven next to him.

"Good God man !" barked Crag, "where did you spring from? I wanted to be alone,to think about Life."

The hookah bubbled, smoke drifted out from between Sven's bandages, as his hand scraped the tragic words ' *HELP ME*' with a piece of chalk across the small blackboard.

Crag's mind raced. At last, a chance to find an answer behind this enigma. He could feel himself becoming energised as he knew Sven could provide part of the answer to the unsolved mystery.

Sven's moving hand scrawled again,'*I NEED A PISS*'

Thwarted again... Crag drew on his rough shag. "Sort yourself out you bandaged addict." he snapped," I want no part of your strange, twisted toilet habits."

'*SCREW YOU!*', was the scribbled reply as Sven trundled off, trailing wispy coils of smoke.

As a disgusted Crag sat adjusting his over-pressed trousers, his thoughts were broken by urgent shouts of 'Man overboard.. Man overboard!..'

He looked over the rail to see a fully clothed figure, face down and motionless, floating away from the side of the ship. As he looked down at the long over-grown fingernails, he knew with a sickening certainty who had just taken their last swim with the fishes

Chapter 23. Murder

The body was retrieved from the sea by Esmee's tattooed sister Sis.
She had quickly removed her loincloth and halter before diving into the
water with a rope between her teeth. As she struck out strongly towards the
floating body, the onlookers were treated to an exclusive reprise of Lord of
the Rings- Twin Towers as her tattoos became animated, writhing and
crawling over the sun-browned smooth skin. The ageing rock-star seemed
particularly interested in Gollum urgently seeking out his precious.
People helped with the rope as the body was pulled up back on deck. There
were gasps of horror as the bedraggled face of the Anglo-Swedish
industrialist stared back with opaque unblinking eyes.
"Hmm interesting," surmised Crag as he stroked his recently reduced
lantern-jaw and non-existent moustache, "why would the Anglo-Swedish
industrialist go for a swim fully clothed?"
"You belted buffoon!" cried Omah scornfully," he didn't 'go for a a swim'
you fool, he was pushed overboard after being murdered. Look at the
marks on his neck."
They all crowded round and looked at the recently departed industrialist.
His well fed neck had four puncture wounds on the back and side.The
holes were large knitting-needle sized and unevenly spaced.
" You know what this means," snorted Crag.
"Exactly" retorted Omah,"someone wanted to shut him up. Someone on
this ship didn't want him talking - shooting his mouth off. Someone here,
among us - he paused - is a MURDERER!"
The group gasped and started to look nervously around, first of all
avoiding eye contact but eventually looking hard and intensely into each of
their neighbours eyes. Who can I trust? Whose next? Is it me? All eyes
started darting in wild panic. All eyes except Steward's, as he radiated
quiet calm, dispensing liquid fortification to shaking hands.
As the alcohol took effect, the small frightened group stood motionless in a
silent circle, looking at the prone body of the industrialist. It was still
oozing seawater from the sodden clothes and corpse. The unspoken
question - 'Who could do this and why?'- hung over them in the air, silent.
The Griffon, that had been perched on the rail, head cocked, observing this
strange human ritual, threw it's head back and gave a mighty screech.....

Chapter 24. History

Not much was known about the recently departed Anglo-Swedish industrialist.He had obviously been a man of great influence and had interests in many countries, ranging from engineering in Germany to real-estate in Britain. He had also been big in trousers. While the group organised his return to the water - a burial at sea was deemed appropriate - Crag's razor sharp, analytical brain snapped into action. He didn't trust Sven and felt sure he was somehow involved in the murder. He needed to find out more about this mysterious, bandaged figure and soon saw his chance.

The group were discussing how best to perform a funeral at sea. The ageing rock-star was suggesting appropriate guitar solos while Sven was entertaining Esmee with more chalk drawings of genitalia. Crag slipped away unnoticed and made for Svens container.

Crag tried the big steel latch and it was open. He edged carefully inside, closing the door behind him and let his eyes get accustomed to the gloom. A single table lamp, on a desk surrounded by framed photographs provided the only illumination. The general appearance was that of a 1940's Captain's cabin; comfortable and business-like.

The walls were covered with old framed photographs, some faded with time, together with official letters and certificates, some with illuminated manuscript headings. Most of the the pictures reflected a submariner's life in World War II - a life in the *Kriegsmarine* - where young, ambitious officers stood in uniformed, proud lines along various U-boat decks, including the U-57. There were pictures of work-worn, grinning faces from the workers at the Deutsche Werke AG submarine yards at Kiel, together with typed and hand-written messages of congratulation from fellow *Oberleutnants* in the Amsel wolfpack. In pride of place was a framed *Ritterkreuz des Eisernen Kreuzes,* the Knights Cross of the Iron Cross. This was the second highest award in the Third Reich, signed by *Grossadmiral* Karl Donitz and given in recognition of extreme bravery and leadership. It had been awarded to *Oberleutnant* Sven Liesen, commander of U-57, for a mission of extreme daring.

Meanwhile on deck, the funeral had finished and people were beginning to drift away...

Chapter 25. Hide

In Sven's container, Crag had found nothing. Everywhere he looked he saw tributes and memorabilia from a successful career and nothing else. He started leafing urgently through papers and magazines on a coffee-table but could find nothing of interest. There was the usual coffee-table reading, copies of *Submarine Monthly - What Sub? - Reader's Subs - Classic U-Boat* , but no hint as to the real man who lived here.

He was momentarily distracted by a particularly fine fuselage in *Reader's Subs* when he heard the metallic groan of the steel latch. Sven was back. Crag looked around for somewhere to hide and quickly jumped behind a convenient male mannequin which was dressed in the uniform of *oberleutnant*. Crag crouched low as the shambling figure of Sven made it's way over to the desk and sat down heavily with his back to Crag, the dim back light silhouetting Sven's bandaged head.

Crag looked over at the door to make his escape but knew he would immediately be seen and how would he explain why he was there? He had to stay crouched until an opportunity arose for his exit. Meanwhile Sven sat at his desk scratching his bandages and tilting his head,first one way and then the other.

Crag's legs had the cramps and he could hardly move. He would *have* to stand-up soon, the pain was agonising. He was wondering if he could slowly get up and stand close behind the mannequin but he was considerably taller than the *oberleutnant*. Just as he was about to fall over in agony, there was a knock on the steel door and Esmee tripped lightly in.'Sven! you silly old sausage, you left your writing board on-deck,' she trilled,'I hope you don't mind me barging in?'

Sven welcomed her in with effusive hand and arm flourishes as she skipped past Crag's crouched figure and hugged Sven hard. Crag saw this chance to slowly rise up behind the mannequin and stand, hidden behind it. Esmee looked radiant. The light from the table-lamp was showing through her thin mini-dress as she danced like a garden fairy for Sven's pleasure. With a whoop of delight, she pulled the dress off, over her head, and danced and posed naked before him, a grown-up slender pixie, her beautiful body glowing in the lamp light.

Sven's head bobbed from side to side with increasing fervour. Crag was having trouble with his trousers as an unforeseen stimulus had forced them into a huge sideways tent, which was forcing itself into the rear of the mannequined *oberleutnant*. As the *oberleutnant* rocked with the pressure from Crag's tent, Sven's head stopped and turned abruptly. Eyes behind the two slits looked directly into Crag's. He had been seen....

Chapter 26. Sick

Sven sat and stared incredulously at the sight of Crag standing behind the rocking, uniformed mannequin, his hands round it's waist.
'It's to stop it falling over' he blurted, unconvincingly.
'My God' gasped Esmee,' were you spying on us? Is that how you get your kicks? And why are you rogering a MANNEQUIN ??'
Crag searched for excuses, unable to speak. Sven sat dumbfounded, shaking his bandaged head in mournful disbelief. He reached for his chalk and writing-board, started to write, then changed his mind and threw it into a nearby chair in disgust.
Crag looked down to his trousers and was relieved to see the straining tent had subsided but not before it had been witnessed by Esmee and Sven who were looking at him pitilessly.
The three stood motionless in the cabin's gloom, while brave hirsute faces from the past, stared down accusingly from their portraits. A glorious, illustrated past of triumphs and successes now permanently defiled by a pathetic peeping-tom with a penchant for sex with dummies.
Not for the first time, Crag wanted to slither way and hide his shame. How could he explain? They wouldn't understand how it had all been a mistake. He would have to justify his presence and he couldn't without accusing Sven. But accuse him of what exactly? Wearing a head bandage? Making Esmee laugh?
Crag decided, unwisely, to go on the attack. ' So.. you hookah smoking degenerate, how do you explain all the memorabilia cluttering up this room eh?'
'Don't be horrid to him,' admonished Esmee, 'it's not hurting you and these are his things, his memories. He doesn't have to explain it to you anyway.'
Sven who had remained motionless, head bowed, moved over to pick up his chalk and board and slowly scrawled the two words *'MY FATHER'*.
'You mean your father was a dealer in World War II junk?' scoffed Crag.
'No you fool!' scolded Esmee, ' All this was his father's life. Sven's father is the captain in these photos. Sven's father was the captain of U-57. That's his father's *oberleutnant's* uniform you were rogering.'

Crag was developing an uneasy feeling.

For the very first time he could see growing anger in Esmee's eyes. 'You swine!' she spat. 'Not only do you spy on us, you then have to sexually defile the uniform and memory of Sven's brave father. You really are a sicko. Get OUT!'

Crag turned dejectedly and made for the door. As he turned his head back to try for a mumbled, unheard apology, he saw the word '*PEDERAST!*' scrawled on Sven's board....

Chapter 27. Adoption

Crag wandered desolately around the leaning deck of the stricken *Lagos Star*, feeling wretched. His misguided attempt to save the ship had literally gone up in flames, together with his uplifting coiffured hair and manly moustache. All his attempts to woo the woman he idolised, had come to nothing as she now despised him after the peeping-tom, sex with dummy incident.

He'd spent the morning trying to restore his good humour by re-organising his wardrobe. Normally an appraisal of the elegantly presented range of safari suits and cravats would have quickly lifted his spirits but now, he noticed some of the severely pressed creases were less than perfect and his favourite mankini clearly had a soiled gusset. The Steward had been called and dispatched with his laundry tasks, effusively retreating with the offending garments, but still Crag felt despondent. His brain returned to the Grand Plan.

As he walked on, his planning was broken by the sound of a loud screech above him. Looking up he saw the Old Bent Crone's container with the Griffon perched on the arm of the Old Bent Crone's wickerwork rocking chair. She was murmuring to the bird whilst stroking it's impressive cruppers.

'That's a handsome bird you have there, old woman,'he offered.

'My second is in Deuteronomy but not in Pipework,' she said with a nod,'leave me alone I know nothing - nothing you hear!'

'Pray madam I mean you no harm.' rejoined Crag in a Dickensian riposte,' I am merely a traveller seeking the truth and many in this fair land have spoken of your beguiling wisdom.'

The old crone cackled, pleased with flattery.'Maybe I do know a thing or two,'she said, ' but some things are best left buried, some mysteries best left unsolved.'

The Griffon had lazily flapped onto Crag's shoulder and was busy pecking and pulling at some exposed shoulder padding.

'Who owns this damn bird,' he snapped,'bloody disgrace! Could do with some proper training.'

'Nobody,' the old crone replied.'Nobody owns it. It belongs to the ship. Now leave me alone! I want to be alone!'

She turned and retreated into the container leaving her chair gently rocking. The Griffon decided it liked its new comfy perch and settled on Crag's shoulder.

Crag and the Griffon looked at each other, eyeball to eyeball…

Chapter 28. Politics

As the days drifted by, Esmee found she actually liked being adrift at sea. It removed her from the constraints of conventional living. The everyday customs and rules of behaviour had been slowly eroded away and she was free to live and behave in a way that reflected her true spirit and desires. Out here in the middle of the ocean, drifting aimlessly, she was free.

She loved spending time catching up with her sister. They had so much to talk about after those lost years. And being a young, attractive woman on a disabled ship where most of the passengers were men, gave her a full social calender. Most evenings, after days spent talking in groups and gazing out to sea, she would find herself in someone's cosy container being entertained until the early hours. She loved the mens' company. Sven was a scream with his sexual drawings and hookah and she loved performing for him, while she always wanted to hear Steward's accounts of his hot, sticky nights spent in the tropics. Omah had a cool effortless sexuality she found addictive, often resulting in unsteady feet as she left his container.

The one exception was the disgraced politician. She didn't know his name and didn't want to. She first met him when he was outside his container polishing an ornate, hand-crafted name plate which hung outside the door and read 'La Maison du Canard'. Apparently after he had fallen from grace, his wife had decided, to avoid further humiliation, that they should emigrate. She had bought tickets for their passage but had failed to turn up at the Tilbury terminal for the sailing departure, texting she would catch him up at the next port of call. After more promissory texts from her, followed by missed dockings, he got the message. He was on his own. Esmee found him an easy person to dislike. Whenever he talked to her he fixed her with reptilian eyes and zoomed in far too close as she caught the odour of half-digested food, mixed with stale cigar. His well-fed face seemed to possess a permanent sheen and his hair featured a combed-over extravaganza which prevented him from any outside activities on windy days.

Worst of all was his habit of resting his hand on Esmee's bottom as he talked to her. She had no problem with open flirting and touching - she liked it - but she disliked the sly, proprietary way his hand suggested ownership.

When he wasn't exploring with his hand, the ex-MP spent his days canvassing the other passengers into the need for committees and advisory panels and the requirement for a home-rule referendum for the *Lagos Star*, where he would reluctantly stand as Chancellor should the public request it. Usually his parliamentary pronouncements were met with undisguised yawns or silence which sadly deprived him of his reason for existing. Without an audience - his oxygen and life blood - he often retreated, disappointed, to his container, much to Esmee's relief.

She hadn't spoken to Crag since the rear-sex-with-dummy incident. She was still annoyed at the violation but was beginning to soften as she watched him lonely in his daily, friendless trudge, wandering around the decks, while the Griffon, still firmly clamped to his shoulder, pecked at the sprouting tufts of padding and emerging hair...

Chapter 29. Clues

Crag meanwhile was busy with his master plan to save the ship. He'd calculated that the store of everyday fertiliser in handy sacks, next to the ex-Army faulty detonators, could be used to re-start the engines and get the ship moving.

As he grappled with the formulae of quantum physics necessary for the correct application of the rudiments of combustion, he had to endure annoying, constant sniping from Omah.

' Ah, the Master Mechanic ' Omah drawled, deliberately stroking his luxuriant, still present moustache, 'so who are you now with that bird? A pirate? Long John Silver? That bird must be very attached to you.' Omah giggled to himself.

Crag fumed in silence. The bird was indeed *very* attached. Each time Crag attempted to remove it from his shoulder, the grip of it's eight, sharp, powerful claws intensified, digging deep into his flesh, causing him agonising pain. Also the bird's cruppers were growing larger which increased the level of discomfort. Oh how he wished he could free himself from this pesky Griffon.

'It's nothing,' he rejoined lightly, I like the company, you should try it.

'No thanks,'laughed Omah,'I prefer women on my shoulder, much more fun.Do you like women Long John? Or do you bat for the other side? Or perhaps you're still a virgin eh?'

Crag tried not to show his humiliation by adjusting his trouser creases but Omah had touched a very raw nerve. By a series of mishaps and misunderstandings, Crag was indeed still ignorant in the ways of a woman. He was certainly keen to explore the sexual world but a combination of bad timing, over excitement and lack of self-control had, so far denied him this pleasure.

The Griffon - bored by Crag's company - loosened it's grip and slowly flapped off to find a more interesting perch.

A relieved Crag made his way down to the hold to check the components for his combustible plan. As he was about to round a corridor he heard voices. He stopped in his tracks and peered cautiously round the corner to see Sven and the Old Bent Crone deep in murmured conversation. Crag could see Sven holding his bandages open. *So Sven can talk after all!* He edged closer, straining to overhear the conversation.

'Blah,Blah,Blah...accident in 1943, Blah,Blah... special cargo. Blah,Blah... Monk Thought...Blah,Blah...revenge...'.

Suddenly they stopped talking. *'Shh! I heard someone..'*

Crag started to whistle loudly and strolled casually past the couple giving a cheery wave and trying hard to look relaxed. Inside his head though, his thoughts were reeling…

Chapter 30. Tent

Crag made his way back to the container, stunned by what he'd just heard. It had only been snippets but enough to confirm his suspicions. There was something linking people on the ship but he couldn't see the connection. As he opened the door, Esmee was standing in her knickers sponging some stains off her dress.

'Oh! I.. I'm sorry,'blurted an embarrassed Crag, 'I'll come back later.'
'It's alright silly,' she giggled,'I don't mind if you don't. You like looking don't you?'

Crag sat down cautiously his hands crossed over his trousers as he felt the familiar re-organisation of his gusset. He tried to avoid looking at her as she sang quietly to herself but was entranced by her beauty, standing there almost naked. His trousers were beginning to strain alarmingly, he tried thinking of late Planning Applications but to no avail. His voice became a croak.'I overheard Sven talking to the Old Bent Crone, there's a conspiracy of silence on this ship and they're part of it.'

'Mmm, interesting,' murmured Esmee,' so what part does the great detective think I play in this conspiracy? Am I the murderer? Or perhaps I'm the innocent bystander?'

'Oh no,' rushed Crag, ' I'm not accusing you - sorry if I gave that impression.'

'That's good,' she murmured,' so let's be friends again,' and she slowly walked over to him, knelt down and looked into his eyes.

As he gazed into her warm, inviting eyes, then stared at her breasts, he felt the familiar, un-stoppable rush as his trousers jerked in release, signalling another laundry job for the Steward...

Chapter 31. Stain

'You're becoming a regular customer sir,' intoned the Steward as he sponged Crag's stained trousers, 'I'm glad my valeting services can be of help.

'Yes ,thanks,' replied an embarrassed Crag.' 'fraid I had an accident with some chicken soup, spilled the stuff over my lap, bloody nuisance eh?'
'Quite so sir,' smirked the Steward, 'that err *chicken soup* can certainly cause a few problems in the trouser department. Have you ever tried, ahem, taking your time and saving it for the main course?'

'Soup for the main course?' queried Crag, 'I'm not sure I know what you mean.'

'Oh I think you do sir. I might be able to help. When I worked on a yacht in the Tropics, my then employer had a similar problem, he found it helped to think about me.'

'You!?' barked Crag, 'why the hell would I want to think of you?'

'Well you see sir, whenever he felt as if he might prematurely spill some "*chicken soup*" , he used to imagine I was there standing in the room. It always worked for him. Sometimes he asked me to actually stand in the room and watch - in fact he preferred it - said it saved him having to imagine.'

Crag was flabbergasted. 'You mean you stood there watching while your employer and his good lady partook of hiding the sausage?'

'A crude term but yes sir, I enjoyed being of service, occasionally they asked me to join in.'

Crag had heard enough. 'Enough of this perverse sexual banter Steward, I'm off for a healthy bracing walk on deck. Don't forget to severely press those trousers.'

'Of course sir, the creases will be knife-sharp. And if you would like my assistance with Esmee, I'll be happy to oblige…'

Chapter 32. Sis

Esmee's sister, Sis looked down at her hard, muscular, brown body and gently sighed. She wasn't exactly ashamed of how she looked, most of the time she enjoyed the power it gave her. In fact being able to overcome tough men in a fight had been very rewarding. She had spent years cage-fighting in the sleazier parts of Phnom Penh, where she had perfected her combat technique. The fight promoters, always looking for sensation, had paid her extra for fighting men. The regular prize money had more than paid for her lifestyle and splendid tattoos as well as a considerable nest-egg, which she had managed to turn into a small fortune on Wall St. by suggesting physical harm to a series of male brokers.

But sometimes she missed being a normal, slender, feminine woman like her sister.

She hadn't always looked like this. Before the accident in the Hadron Collider she had looked much like Esmee - petite, fair and delicate. When the accident had turned her into anti-matter with her atomic particles beaming into the atmosphere, something had happened on re-entry - a rogue-male gene atom in the stream perhaps - which had left her physically bigger, taller, tough and strong.

She still had the good looks and shape of a woman, but a woman of massive Amazonian proportions. She stood at well over six feet, had broad shoulders, beautiful breasts and child-bearing hips. Her legs were long and heavily muscled as was her upper-arms. A brave man she had once slept with, had said it was like making love to an annoyed crocodile.

She didn't like Crag, thinking him a self-obsessed, weak buffoon but in truth, as a result of her years spent cage-fighting, she had formed that decision about most men.

However she was intrigued by his seemingly idiotic quest for the truth. He seemed to be obsessed with a conspiracy mystery surrounding the people on board ship. She had to admit that even by her standards they were a strange bunch. An alleged son of a U-boat commander who spent his drugged, bandaged time drawing genitalia on a black-board. The internationally renowned actor and card player Omah Sharif, an Old Bent Crone, a recently dispatched Anglo-Swedish industrialist, a disgraced MP, an ageing rock-star and of course the mysterious Steward who always seemed to appear, when needed, as if on cue. She made up her mind to quiz Crag, to find out what was driving his bizarre, investigative mind and perhaps slap him around a bit…

Chapter 33. Pain

It had been a rough night on board the *Lagos Star*. High winds and rain had lashed the rusty decks, causing some of the containers to shift, adding to the ship's lack of stability. Ever since Crag's attempt to re-start the engines , and the subsequent explosion, the ship had developed an alarming list to port which was now much more significant after the night's gales.

Crag was inspecting the previous night's damage, pipe clenched firmly, lantern jaw grimly set, when his immediate surroundings grew dark with the shadow of Sis looming over him. He gulped as he looked up and saw her standing over him, arms akimbo, legs apart.

'Just checking for damage,'he announced officially,' the old tub took a battering last night, eh?'

'Save the cliches for my sister,' she shot back,' and is it possible for you to speak to me normally or can you only speak in that pathetic hero talk?
'Err..umm steady-on old thing,' he retorted,'just trying to keep chin-up, eh what?'
'You're a ridiculous excuse for a man, a sad, pulp-fiction throwback. How on earth do you manage to even wipe your own arse?'
Crag was not used to being talked to like this and was starting to feel aggrieved. 'Now look here,' he began,' I like a bit of banter just like the next man but totty should know their place, eh?'

When he came round, his head was painfully throbbing and one arm and a leg felt very sore indeed. His freshly pressed safari trousers were down around his ankles and the pipe had been fully inserted into a very personal orifice.
'You were saying..?' she said with a withering look, as she absent-mindedly played with her glossy, black hair, twisting it round her fingers.
'Nothing.. nothing at all,' he blurted, 'just a joke eh?'
He reached down, carefully withdrawing his re-located pipe and almost put it back in his mouth before stopping himself. Painfully pulling up his trousers, he was convinced either his arm, or leg, or both were broken. He looked up at her with a new respect, born out of fear.
'So, you pathetic worm, tell me about this so-called conspiracy theory you've been spouting off about, before I decide to *really* hurt you....'

Chapter 34. Dim

As Crag started to tell Sis about his suspicions he found his eyes wandering lasciviously over her body-art. Her tattoos mesmerised him, he was fascinated by the exciting tableaux before him. Unfortunately Sis was not in the mood to be ogled at -particularly by this creep - and had to remind him, with the odd, hard slap, that he needed to keep to his story.
He started at the beginning, his bad day at the office followed by his and Esmee's surreal evening at the pub in Gloomworth when things had got out of hand and they had found themselves on this container ship. He was keen to point out to Sis that at all times he had been in masterful control of the situation. She doubted that was the case, but at least he had kept Esmee safe during their exploits, out of harm's way.

Sis became interested when Crag described the overheard conversation between the Old Bent Crone and Sven. She had to admit something about the pair didn't sound right.

'So, what do you think the accident was in 1943?' she asked.

'Search me,' said Crag, ' but it was in wartime, World War II, so must have been around the time Sven's father was commander of the U-boat.

'If it *was* Sven's father, and has anybody seen his face without those bandages?'

'Hells Teeth! 'he exclaimed, ' you don't mean..'

'Exactly, we don't know anything about Sven, he could be anybody. There's only his word.'

'Mmm..interesting,'mused Crag as he filled his pipe with some more rough shag obtained for him by his trusted lackey off the Burlington Arcade,'so the chap could be a complete fraud?'

'Bingo, my feeble friend, and what about you? Are you who you say you are?'

Crag was feeling decidedly uneasy. 'Of course.. damn cheek.. ,are you suggesting I'm involved in some sort of skulduggery?'

'Relax big man, no offence . You're too dim to be duplicitous.'

Crag drew heavily on his pipe, feeling flattered…

Chapter 35. Pleased

In the dim, warm light of his cosy container, Sven sat back in his armchair feeling very pleased with himself. Perhaps it was the aromatic exhilaration from the hookah, making his brain sparkle with pleasurable sensations or perhaps the recent presence of the delightful and exciting Esmee who had just left, giggling and dancing her way out of his door after hours of flirtatious and sensual fun.

As he eased the tight bandage around his neck and mouth he reminisced on his feverish work with the chalk-board, drawing more and more graphic sexual images, while she had danced naked in front of him, in total, lustful abandon. Oh how he would have loved to have torn the bandages off, kissed her and told her of his lust and desires.

But he couldn't - he never could. She would never be allowed see his face or hear his voice. Everything he'd worked towards would be finished.

Those careful years of planning would have been for nothing. As he let the lazy smoke drift upwards, he looked up at the walls of faded photographs and letters and breathed a sigh of relief. That fool Crag had nearly spoiled everything by snooping around. Luckily the man had been too stupid to see what was in front of his face. Sven let his gaze fall on the *Buchstabe von Commendation* - Letter of Commendation - from *Grossadmiral* Karl Donitz highlighting the bravery shown during Operation Quadriga and remembered the prize at stake.

Meanwhile, in another part of the ship, Steward was humming to himself whilst busy with Crag's trousers, removing some more stains and expertly pressing knife-sharp creases. He was also very pleased with progress, as everything seemed to be falling nicely into position with the plan taking perfect shape...

Chapter 36. Rock

It was another full day for Paul, the ageing rock-star. After a midday breakfast, followed by the first joint of the day, it was time to practice. Paul's container was a shrine to rock, with two rows of guitars hanging from their hallowed places on the walls, ready to be taken down, polished, tuned - and played. He had built up quite a collection to choose from, ranging from a nearly new Flying-V to older vintage Fenders and Gibsons, each one having played it's part in creating the unique sounds and glorious, soaring solos on his seven top-selling albums.
Today was the turn of the cherry red Gibson Melody-Maker made in '64, before Gibson went corporate. He lovingly removed it from its hanging place and carefully dusted the lacquered body and frets, remembering the history behind each scratch and surface chip. It was possibly his all-time favourite. Sure it sometimes felt prehistoric next to the newer, slicker, high-tech guitars in his collection but that sound! It could change instantly from the raw, bluesy, aggressive edge to an almost acoustic delicacy with a deft flick of the tone switch. It was this guitar that had featured extensively on the 'Art Attack' album - the notoriously difficult second album - that had gone on to give Paul his first platinum. He plugged in his powerful practice amp and rolled himself another joint.
Life suited him on this ageing container ship. Much like himself it had been through some hair raising scrapes but survived more or less intact. Time had taken it's toll, with a few knocks around the edges and the odd war-wound, but nothing serious. He took a deep toke and let his mind drift

back to the past. His fourth marriage had not been a success, with music taking centre stage and his wife citing the stage as co-respondent. It was a fact that it was the only time he felt truly alive - there under the hot, blazing lights - with the crowd urging him on and the sound so loud from the bass and drums, it would vibrate your guts, while the sound mix, blasting back at him from the stage monitors would be the best stereo system, ever.

The ship had been his greasy lawyer's idea. He'd persuaded him that to avoid crippling back-tax bills and hungry creditors, his best option was to be state-less, where he could stay out of authority's - and law-courts - way. In fact, become a complete non-person in the eyes of the law. Shortly after his lawyer had given him this advice and set things up, he had moved in with Paul's ex-wife, but Paul did not stay bitter for long. In his heart he knew she hadn't been happy with him. Now, here, on his own, he'd grown to like the other misfits on the ship, where he could play his guitars and reminisce all day with no interruptions.

He switched on the guitar amp, revelling - as always -in the distinctive valve power hum coming from the speaker. He flicked on the drum machine with its warm, red glow, adjusted the volume and blasted his first chord of the session....

Chapter 37. The MP

It was late afternoon as the disgraced Member of Parliament decided on an invigorating promenade. There'd been no one around to hear his latest pronouncements which left him feeling somewhat downcast, so a brisk walk along the deck was called for. He was thinking he might even meet someone who would be interested in his latest ideas on an all-party committee to discuss the rate of water the ship was taking on. Until then, a cigar would be the perfect companion. He snapped the end off a Romeo & Juliet and after several matches and much puffing it was burning nicely. Despite his firm belief in his own staggering intellect and a strong, excessive conviction as a natural public figure and leader, he sometimes felt his career was not progressing as planned. Being adrift on a disabled container ship, shunned by the other misfits on board and sent packing by his wife did not add to his confidence. As he strolled purposefully along the decks he pondered how he had arrived at this sorry state.

It had all started so well, an expensive private education, an average degree, followed by a spell in the family law-firm. But it wasn't enough. His ego demanded a wider audience than the courts and it was easy enough - with the right connections - to be selected to run for a safe seat. Once he was in parliament, the power was almost tangible. Sure the financial corporations and big-business *really* ran things but the pretence was what mattered. The pretence of managing the country coupled with the life-giving oxygen of TV interviews, discussing political dogma and airing opinions. And, of course, the glamorous, expensive lifestyle, paid for by taxpayers. He and his fellow colleagues had become so bloated and insulated by the years of privilege and power he had failed to grasp the countrys' mood. The public - already hardened by a badly judged decision for war - wanted blood when a leaked document revealed extensive corruption in the ranks of their public representatives. He had been found out - openly disgraced. He had to resign, along with many of his pals. His engagements became less, the dinner-parties dwindled, he became a pariah in the social circles he had previously inhabited.

In his mind he felt harshly judged and somewhat bitter as he puffed on his cigar and gazed out to sea, completely unprepared for the sharp tug behind him, as his coat was lifted over his head, his legs grappled together and lifted off the deck. The last thing he remembered was soaring blind, through the air, arms outstretched as he hit the water and felt the roaring water engulf his ears and lungs…

Chapter 38. Respect

'*Doop doop doop,another one bites the dust,*' sang Omah as he sat in the sun outside his container, drinking and working on a new card trick,'*another one bites, another one bites, another one bites the dust.*'
As Crag walked past, he was annoyed by Omah's lack of sensitivity after the murder of the disgraced MP. He didn't like Omah very much, in fact disliked him intensely, and thought he could at least show the recently deceased some respect.
'Can't you behave decently and act accordingly after the MP's demise?' he muttered as he stopped.
'Cool it Batman or is it Robin today,' sneered Omah as he looked Crag up and down, 'the man's dead, whatever song I choose to sing. Why don't you

try slackening off those trousers occasionally and stop acting so high and mighty, Mr ever-so tightly buttoned-up.'

At the mention of his trousers Crag was immediately overcome with awkward and acute embarrassment. He knew full well the Steward had been less than discrete when discussing Crag's laundry requirements with other members of the ship's company. He'd overheard on more than one occasion, others sniggering about the regular stains that appeared around his fly that needed heavy sponging. And he was getting tired with constant jokes, directed at him, about moving to Staines.

He left Omah to finish his bottle of Bulgarian Cava and moved out of earshot where he stopped to refill his pipe with the ready rubbed rough shag (obtained by the same obsequious little drone near the Burlington Arcade) and pondered developments.

There were now only eight left on the stricken ship - nine if you counted that drat Griffon - and one of them must be the murderer. Unless there was someone else on board, as yet undiscovered…

Chapter 39. Militia

The grey dawn was broken by a new, alien sound of thudding rotor blades, as a military style helicopter circled overhead . The ship's inhabitants slowly emerged into the misty, damp morning from the safety of their individual containers and stared upwards, bleary eyed and confused as the big 'copter circled the ship in a continuous, angled sweep. It was coming so close they could see the pilot's Ray-Bans. He was a large black man wearing a camouflage military-style uniform and beret. Next to him, his co-pilot also dressed in camouflage was holding a large automatic weapon, pointing directly down, aiming towards the confused group standing on deck.

A loud-speaker burst into life from the cockpit, "YOU ARE TRESPASSING IN THE WATERS OF THE MILITARY ZONE OF THE SOVEREIGN STATE OF ONTOGO. LEAVE THIS AREA IMMEDIATELY OR WE WILL OPEN FIRE."

The group on deck froze with fear. Crag decided on English diplomacy. 'I say old chap,' he shouted, his voice immediately drowned out by the helicopter's engines, ' we're British subjects and require you treat us under international convention.'

A line of bullets strafed across the deck causing the group to dive for cover as the noise from the helicopter grew to a thunder and it's down-draft started flicking objects around effortlessly like a tornado, scattering them in all directions. It was impossible to see anything or stand upright. The helicopter was going to attempt to land.

Fortunately the sloping list of the damaged ship was proving difficult for the pilot. There wasn't a proper helicopter landing pad and he was trying to land on the angled tops of several containers but the risk of sliding off into the sea deterred him. After several attempts he gave up and hovered stationary above.

"YOU ARE IN VIOLATION. WE HAVE DISPATCHED A GUNBOAT TO SINK YOU.. GOODBYE.." and with a final burst of automatic fire from the grinning co-pilot, the big machine lifted up, hovered for moment, then wheeled away skywards.

As silence returned, the paralysed group stood in fright on the the sloping deck, waiting for the the inevitable. Suddenly a massive jolt juddered through the old ship and they felt a new sensation of vibration and then, movement...

Chapter 40. Moving

The ship was on the move again, righting itself and moving under it's own steam. The group looked over the side and saw the strong, powerful bow-wave, curling and streaming outwards as the ship turned in a wide arc, circling away from danger and heading back out to sea. Behind them, a foaming, turbulent wake, taking them further away from the dangerous waters with every thrash of the giant propellers.

Crag and Omah raced up the walkways to the bridge and were astounded to see the Steward and Sven, confidently manoeuvring controls, cancelling alarms and punching in various commands on control panels.

'What's going on old man?' drawled Omah,' how on earth did you get all this stuff going?'

'Well - ahem,' announced the Steward, ' we have Esmee's sister, Sis to thank for this. Last night she hard-wired the Navigational and Engineering computer via the main generator buzz bars. She then changed the computer's software, which allowed the ancillary power supply to be re-directed to the main drive, giving full servo control. We are now fully operational with all engines, pumps and GPS navigation systems working normally. Once we've finished entering our co-ordinates, this ship will be able to drive itself on auto-pilot. Right now, Sis is down in the engine room, finishing off some cabling.'

'Hmm, not bad for a woman,' mused Crag. Omah and Sven both looked sharply at him, then at each other and shook their heads collectively in disbelief.'

'You really are a piece of work, you idiot,' shouted Omah, 'if I do remember, your attempts to start the engines resulted in chaos, with the ship fire-damaged and taking on water.'

Crag nervously adjusted his trousers,' well err..'

'Shut up you fool,' snapped Omah. 'Go and do something useful like cleaning out the toilets... If you can manage without blowing them up.'

'If I may interject, sir,'announced the Steward,' after some tea, we really should be making plans for our continued journey. Perhaps we could organise a discussion with the others as to where that journey should be…?'

Chapter 41. Meeting

Some sat around the small formica table and others sat awkwardly on the bunk-bed in the departed Captain's cabin. There were eight of them crowded into the small, scruffy room which had stayed unused since the Captain's disappearance. The room was made smaller by shelves on three sides containing instruction manuals, reference books with charts and stacked magazines. The Captain had obviously been a heavy smoker as everything was tinged with yellow, the previously white painted walls and ceiling, now carrying the heavy shade of nicotine.

The Captain's cabin had been chosen as a fitting venue to discuss the future journey. Somehow - despite the tired scruffiness around them - it was felt that decisions reached here would carry more weight , a sort of collective, executive gravitas to be respected and adhered too.

Actually there were nine present; counting the Griffon, which had been brought in by the Old Bent Crone. She sat self-consciously on the edge of the bunk and whispered to the bird while gently stroking it's cruppers.

Crag who had positioned himself prominently at the table, eyed the bird with suspicion.

The Steward busied himself serving everyone drinks and then spoke.

'Ahem, if I could have your attention Ladies and Gentlemen. As we all know this journey has been fraught with disaster. Three of our company have met with untimely deaths. The Captain strangely dissolved in sea-water during swimming, the Anglo-Swedish industrialist died from a mysterious neck injury and the disgraced MP unfortunately met his maker over the side. We have been drifting with no power for months, had a near fatal explosion - *accusing eyes turned to Crag* - and were nearly sunk by a tin-pot African dictatorship. However, due to exemplary work by Sis - *eyes turned to Sis in admiration* - the ship is now in full working order and we are free to continue our journey. As our Global Positioning System is in full working order, I can report we are heading Northwards off the Guinea coast of West Africa. Soon we will need to stop for supplies but the question remains. Where do we go from here..?'

Crag cleared his throat to speak but changed his mind after a penetrating look from Sis.

Sven scrawled the words " *DAKAR FOR SUPPLIES*" on his board.

' Oooh lovely,' trilled Esmee,'Sooo French! and with all those hunky rally drivers too.'

'At last,'sighed Omah,' some real card-action,' as he produced a deck and started to shuffle.

Crag was wondering if his moustache would have grown back sufficiently before they docked...

Chapter 42. Dakar

The co-ordinates had been set and the ship was now ploughing up the African coastline to Senegal where they would be docking for supplies at Dakar. There was an air of quiet anticipation on board at the thought of *terra-firma* and the excitement of the unknown. Their arrival had been scheduled and agreed with the port authorities and the harbour Pilot was booked to steer them in.

Crag was busy selecting only the best of his wardrobe, choosing the pale-blue safari suit with matching cravat, to set foot appropriately on foreign soil. Since the unfortunate 'accident' in the engine room explosion, his hair had begun to grow back but was still a long way from becoming the elaborate coiffured masterpiece he had grown to love. His re-growing moustache had a juvenile appearance next to the luxuriant glossiness of

Omah's, prompting constant suggestions from Omah of '*bum-fluff*' which Crag tried his hardest not to hear.

Esmee was beside herself with joy as she flitted between the group, organising their time on shore. She looked radiant in a fine silk dress given to her by the Old Bent Crone and cleverly altered by Sven to show her body off to it's alluring, perfect best.

They arrived at Dakar the following day, early in the morning. The sea was flat calm, the air still. The city viewed from a distance, looked peaceful, bathed in early morning sunlight, giving the low buildings a soft-focus, light brown glow. Later in the day, the heat from the midday sun would be bleaching the city bone-white.

The ship automatically slowed to a stop outside the harbour entrance and waited for the Pilot who soon arrived in his official looking launch. He quickly scrambled up the rope ladder, shouted something in French to his colleagues who, after a few minutes of dropping him off, revved up the launch and zoomed back into the harbour.

The Pilot, a tall, thin Senegalese with a permanent stoop, wore a tie and shirt with a collar many sizes too big, and an official looking peaked cap. Once the required wad of U.S. Dollars had changed hands he enthusiastically congratulated them on the condition of the vessel and skilfully guided the big ship into position alongside a spare berth, where a group of casual onlookers suddenly sprang into life and made the vessel secure.

The Steward was first down the gang-plank, closely followed Sven, as they went hunting with a shopping list for supplies. A tanker truck had already arrived and was pumping diesel into the ship's tanks, with Sis supervising the operation. One look at Sis's formidable physique, and the tanker operatives had already decided not to short change the *Lagos Star*. Next down the stairway came Paul, the ageing rock-star, resplendent in multi-coloured, tie-dyed Indian cotton and bandanna. An acoustic guitar slung over his shoulder completed the picture as he went on the prowl for music, a woman and some dope.

Esmee, Crag and Omah followed on behind, while the Old Bent Crone - standing on deck - warned them of the perils of staying on-shore too long: 'My third is in Corinthians but not in Sorrow, be back by dawn for we sail tomorrow!' she cackled as the Griffon let out a mighty screech…

Chapter 43. Bar

Omah, Esmee and Crag sat drinking in a back street bar near the docks. The place reminded Omah of a seedier version of *Rick's Bar* in *Casablanca* with it's permanent pall of cigarette smoke but instead of a tinkling pianist, there was the perma-beat of Afro-Arabic and American dance blasting from the juke-box. He was keen to start a card game and earn some money while Esmee looked around flirtatiously at the fit, young men lounging around expectantly. Crag nervously tried adopting a cool pose whilst filling his trusty pipe.

As the drinks started to take effect, Esmee began circling the room, dancing around the swarthy strangers, flirting outrageously. The sexual tension in the air was palpable. Omah had started a card school in a dimly lit corner and was already acquiring a significant pile of crumpled bills as the regular players started viewing him with suspicion.

Crag's pipe was providing his only comfort. He didn't like the way Esmee flirted and showed herself off but he was finding it difficult to concentrate. His normal supply of ready-rubbed rough shag, obtained by his trusty lackey just off the Burlington Arcade had run out and he was now experimenting with some new tobacco, purchased in a rush from a friendly, coloured chap off Brixton High St. He had been mightily impressed with the chap's colourful hat and scarf in red, gold and green. As he puffed away he felt more detached from the party in front of him and failed to notice as the tempo increased. Esmee's loose translation of the Tango was turning into a visceral, swirling frenzy of animal madness. She was laughing and whooping as she relished being thrown between the eager group of young men like a prized rag-doll. Crag was drifting away into oblivion, growing ever more attached to his chair and he failed to notice the subtle change in mood, as the men started to undress Esmee.

It was slowly at first, each taking turns to pull at the thin silk until it started to tear and unravel, but with an increasing fervour until she was dancing in just her underwear. Her mood changed from hilarity to fear as the eager, sweating men started to move in on her but Crag was too distracted to notice, gazing dreamily at the ceiling, listened to the music.

At the same time, Omah's card school erupted in chaos with accusations from the regulars of cheating. It was true that Omah had effectively emptied his card-playing companion's wallets and was now sitting with an enormous pile of banknotes, won fair and square, but the bad losers saw a chance to get their money back.

As the bar exploded into uproar, Esmee was trying to fight off the aroused men while Omah faced the ugly group of disgruntled gamblers who had suddenly produced some sharp looking knives…

Chapter 44. Fight

Things were looking desperate as the mood in the bar was turning primal with the smell of lust and the need for blood. Sex and Revenge - two of the strongest driving forces of the human condition - were high on the agenda. Esmee and Omah were completely outnumbered and Crag was rendered useless, stupefied by the drugs.

As the locals circled like Hyenas, moving in for the kill, the door flew open and Sis stood there tall and strong, back-lit silhouetted by an outside street lamp. She was ready for the fight. The lust crazed males stopped, startled by the intrusion and before they could resume their attack on Esmee, they were instantly, expertly disabled in a series of moves, seen in a slow-motion blur. In a set of jumps, spins and kicks, she left them writhing on the floor, clutching their testicles, howling in pain.

She then moved her attention to the disgruntled gamblers who had now moved over from Omah and were surrounding her, knives flashing. As Sis executed some textbook combat kicks, the knives were scattered, skidding across the floor, lost under tables. The gamblers, enraged beyond endurance, advanced on her with hands ready to tear her apart but using her cage-fighting prowess of chops and throws, they were soon effortlessly dispatched to different corners of the room, lying prone, barely conscious. One of the would-be rapists had sufficiently recovered to try a single attack on Sis and he came running towards her, his leg raised to kick. She grabbed the outstretched leg and twisted her body round. The entire bar heard the sickening crack of a breaking fibula and knee-joint as the man fell to the floor - a collapsed marionette with cut strings.

Esmee was feeling wretched, standing in her underwear sobbing as Omah found a coat and draped it over her shoulders. Sis held her tightly ,whispering comforting words as they made for the door.

'Hey, what about me ?' demanded Crag, still in a semi-stupor. 'Don't leave me here with this lot.'

'Why not,' retorted Sis,'it's what you deserve you pathetic coward. How could you just sit there and let those awful things happen to Esmee? You WORM!'

How could Crag explain about the strange 'tobacco' without making things worse. He could only hope the incident would eventually be forgotten so he meekly followed behind, like a scolded dog, as they all made their way back to the ship....

Chapter 45. Hugs

The four of them made a strange quartet as they made their way wearily through the back-streets of Dakar's dockland. Omah and Sis were supporting a still shaking Esmee who's nakedness was covered by a stranger's coat many sizes too big. Crag following sheepishly behind. He looked like a ridiculous colonial throwback with his light blue safari suit and cravat. Why did things always go wrong for him? Not for the first time he felt foolish and humiliated.

The streets were deserted and the sun was beginning to come up as they reached the dockside and saw the welcoming shape of the *Lagos Star* towering over them. As they walked up the gangway they saw the Steward, busy with Sven, checking the newly arrived pallets of supplies. Steward was shocked when he saw Esmee.

'My God, Esmee, what happened..?

'Oh just a little local difficulty,' explained Sis, 'she'll tell you later. Some good news from Omah though.'

Omah beamed, his dark eyes twinkling as he pulled enormous wads of cash from each of his pockets.'Bit of luck on the tables old man, this should keep us going for a while eh?'

The group laughed and congratulated Omah on his success, with Sven's heavily bandaged head bobbing from side to side in enthusiasm.

'Are we all here?' asked Sis.

'Just waiting for rock-star Paul.' said the Steward,'Ah.. here he is now.'

They looked down to the quay as Paul arrived accompanied by two statuesque African beauties, all three, arm-in-arm and laughing. With elaborate hugs and kisses they finally parted company and Paul swaggered up the gangway, waving down to them as they shouted their farewells.

As Paul stood on deck joking with the others, he suddenly realised he actually felt happy. For the first time, for as long as he could remember, he felt he belonged somewhere. Among this strange group of floating misfits, he was content and had a place he could call home.

'Right then...Let's get this show on the road,' he announced, as the others smiled their approval…

Chapter 46. Collar

With supplies stored aboard and the engines primed, the ship was ready to cast-off for the next stage of the journey. They had decided to carry on up Africa's west coast, enjoying the good weather but as yet they had not agreed the final destination. It was a game of cat and mouse, where several mice and a few of the cats had their own secret agendas. As time had passed however, friendships had been made and loyalties strengthened which had played havoc with some of the more dastardly individual plans. Exactly on time, the Senegalese Pilot came striding along the quay to take command - and relieve them of several hundred US Dollars - to pilot the ship out beyond the harbour walls.

As Paul and Omah watched him climb on board they both commented on his shirt and tie, specifically the collar, which seemed to have visibly grown since his last visit. He was the same thin, scrawny man, his neck stretched and taut but the shirt collar seemed to rest on his shoulders rather than the neck. The extra large circumference of the collar - clearly meant for a giant of a man - meant most of the tie was fully concealed, which resulted in a comical, short, stubby knot with a few inches of visible tie to grace his shirt front. The jaunty angle of the official looking peak-cap - which could have been bought at any sea front beach shop - completed the slightly bizarre ensemble.

However his control of the ship was masterful, the massive propellers throwing churning foam against the dockside while the mighty vessel eased away from the quay, with fond shouts and farewells from the dock workers. The onboard group could only marvel as he manoeuvred the ship as casually as if it were a small river launch, spinning and manipulating the controls with a speed that, at times, seemed to make the ship pirouette.

Soon the *Lagos Star* was back outside the harbour entrance where they were joined by the Pilot's launch which raced alongside. The Pilot wished them well, shook hands vigorously, gave them a dog-eared business card of his brother's restaurant in Casablanca and disappeared down the rope ladder to the waiting launch and was gone.

Sven and the Steward, who seemed to have assumed joint Captainship, set the ship's Navigational GPS for Tangier, nodded to each other and left the bridge to the expert control of the computer.

The ship surged forward, slicing through the cobalt sea towards it's next adventure...

Chapter 47. Sven

With the ship ploughing a strong and steady course, the return of the familiar sounds and vibrations pleased Sven as he wandered back to his container. He opened the big steel door, went in locking it behind him and slumped into his favourite chair, relieved his plan was still on track...Or was it? Over the last few months he had grown close to the other misfits on board and he was beginning to doubt his resolve. He moved over to the dressing table, sat in front of the mirror and began to unravel his head bandages.

As he unwound the lengths of surgical crepe he studied, for the umpteenth time, the face being revealed and hated what he saw. The skin without it's exposure to sun and air had taken on a grey pallor and was corpse-like in appearance but it was the face itself which really repulsed him. The surgery had been a complete disaster. He had been promised a new face, one which nobody would recognise and in a way it was true. It had been botched in such a way which had pulled it out of shape, giving it a lopsided look, his mouth sloping sideways and slack jawed, his left eyelid permanently drooping, half-closed.

As he studied the face looking back at him from the mirror, he was reminded of a severe stroke victim. Why had he done this to himself?...Money of course, it was always about money...What else?

He had been brought up in the Weberwiese area of East Berlin in a small, two bedroom rented apartment off Karl-Marx-Allee. The block of apartments, like much of East Berlin, was built in the late '50s as a depressing tribute to Stalin's un-inspiring style of architecture. His family had always been poor, his father had disappeared early on - destination unknown - his mother never discussing it. She worked hard as a cleaner in one of the state Stasi buildings, bringing up three children on her own as best she could. Sven was the eldest child, with a younger brother and then his little sister. For some reason his brother and sister accepted the life given to them and grew up fairly happy with few emotional scars but he hated it. He hated the daily struggle to make ends meet. He hated the baiting and bullying at school which he felt was due to the family's poverty and was determined to escape as soon as he could....

Chapter 48. Scam

Sven sucked on his hookah-pipe in the cosy container, letting the smoke drift up to the ceiling and listened to the drone of the ship's engines. He let his mind drift back to earlier days and reflected on his teenage years.
He had left school with no qualifications and drifted through a selection of poorly paid jobs in an effort to help out with the family finances but found the constant poverty was eating away at him. There were often rows - usually started by him - around the dinner table, which upset his mother, brother and sister. They couldn't understand why he was always so restless and sad. As a fatherless family they were poor but they shared the simple joy of their lives together. A struggling family but happy in each other's company but Sven never felt he belonged. Eventually, after a particularly unpleasant row, he stormed out with his few meager possessions and moved into a small flat nearby, sharing with an ex-schoolfriend where he was able to contribute towards the rent and still give some money to his mother.
He had just turned twenty-seven when the Berlin Wall came down in a fanfare of celebrations. Amid the chaos, the city began the long road to re-unification and he soon realised this could be a time of opportunity. His flatmate Carl worked in a insurance office in Alexanderplatz and used to tell him about the new money that was flooding in from the West. Sven used to listen intently to Carl's tales of money that was paid out in claims, some of them fraudulent.
One evening after dinner, Carl was telling Sven about his day and what had happened.' A million Mark payout, what I could do with a million.'
Sven looked up. 'A million? What for?'
Carl thought for a moment. 'Life insurance. The guy disappeared. His wife got the money after two years. He was insured for a million.'
'Didn't they check things out - before handing it over?'
'Oh sure... You bet for a million? Even the police were used. But in the end, no body, no proof and the rules say, after a two year period, if nothing floats to the surface - if you get my drift - we pay out.'

Sven turned the possibilities over in his head and at that point in his young life, he formulated a plan that would be his downfall... A future destroyed...Just for money...

Chapter 49. Fraud

Sven sat in his chair and pondered on the confidence of youth. He thought back to those years when he had been a brash young man, naive enough to think he could out-smart an insurance company.

He had figured that in the chaos of re-unification, he could engineer his own disappearance and using a fictitious name and next of kin, would claim his own life insurance. To allay superstition, he promptly left the shared apartment and using a deceased person's name, acquired new western identity papers and another flat. Using another deceased name, found from a cemetery, he built up an entirely fictitious brother living in Hannover who loved him so much that he took out life insurance on him for a million Deutschmarks.

Twice a week Sven took the train from Berlin to Hannover where he walked to the empty, rented flat he used to communicate with the insurance company. Most days there were letters on the door-mat requesting information for their files, even one requesting his doctor's address which he quickly had to set up. After a few months, all was in place, the company had accepted the insurance risk. All he had to do was wait until the time was right.

After a year, the insurance company received a distraught letter from the fictitious brother in Hannover claiming his other brother had gone missing during a boating holiday. Around the same time Sven found a struck-off alcoholic surgeon in the former East Berlin who agreed to perform the face surgery , with no questions asked, to give Sven a new face .

The pain after the operation - performed on a kitchen table in a seedy flat - was excruciating but eventually, after several months, it subsided. He was assured the new face would look fine after the initial trauma but it never did. The lop-sided look was there for keeps. Eventually he moved and took up permanent residence in the Hannover flat as the grieving brother of the missing person.

Over the next two years he received constant calls and visits from enquiry agents, the police and officials from the insurance company but he always managed to hold his composure and finally, after three difficult years, they agreed to pay compensation but only a twentieth of the insured sum, due to what they called *'suspicious circumstances'* . Sven was distraught. The four and a half years rental of the two apartments, the constant commuting and the expensive, botched plastic surgery had cost him dear and the fifty thousand marks barely covered the expenses. However he knew the insurance people had long had their suspicions, so all he could do was take the money offered, without a fuss.

He was finally left alone, a lonely, anonymous identity, in an anonymous town with no friends and little money. He had a family whom he would never be able to see or make contact with again and a face that could frighten children.

Sven was too embarrassed by his appearance to venture out much. Whenever he did he wrapped his face in a scarf and wore a hat, pulled low over his brow. He filled his lonely days walking in the local park, or when it was cold, visiting the museum. One raw winter's day in the warmth of the museum's reading room he found himself engrossed in the story of a U-boat that went missing during World War II. His interest grew into an obsession and became the reason he was now sitting in a metal box on the *Lagos Star* container ship, wrapped in bandages, surrounded by memorabilia from the *Kreigsmarine* submariner's navy and more specifically, the U-57…

Chapter 50. Advice

Crag sat on deck watching the horizon, puffing on his pipe which he'd primed with some African rough shag obtained by a new trusted lackey just off the Dakar bazaar. He was relieved to find that, despite it's rough, raw edge, which gave him a hacking cough, it didn't play games with his brain like the previous stuff. Never again would he buy his tobacco in Brixton. He frowned as he smoothed the creases in his safari trousers and toyed with his freshly clipped moustache.

His popularity was at all time low. He'd managed to alienate most of the people on board and was now being actively shunned by Esmee. Women eh? Crag just couldn't fathom where he was going wrong and need some advice, but who could he go to? The men on board regarded him as a figure of fun, making jokes at his expense. As for the women, he was embarrassed to admit that in addition to finding it difficult to discuss personal matters, he found he always grew a huge erection whenever he was near to Esmee or Sis. Whichever way he twisted or squirmed, the huge tent in his trousers was always highly visible and the cause of much hilarity with the girls.

The only other woman on the ship he could try talking to was the Old Bent Crone. Summoning his emotional strength he made his way warily along the walkway to her container where she sat in her usual position, outside, gently rocking in her wickerwork chair.

'Hello old woman and how do I find you on this fair morning?' he quipped.

'My third is in paintwork but not in strawberry,' she muttered,' what do you want from me?.. I am but a poor defenceless old woman.'

As Crag re-ran their previous conversations in his mind, he realised he was wasting his time but carried on.

'Pray old woman, I mean you no harm. Rather that I should come to you for your great wisdom and knowledge, which is legend.'

The Old Bent Crone cackled. 'Very well then, make your point before I tire of this wordy jest.'

Hesitantly Crag started. 'Well..Umm, the problem is I'm not very good with women. I have never, err, known the feminine ways of a woman.'

'Ah so you're still a virgin - at your age too!' at which point she nearly fell out of her rocking chair with hysterical laughter.

'Virgin..Virgin.' The words echoed around Crag's head as he left the cackling crone, rocking feverishly in her chair. When would he ever be able to rid himself of this curse? When would he be able to call himself a *real* man? He remembered the time when Esmee had wanted him to take her roughly but he'd prematurely failed and now she regarded him with pity. He thought about Sis. Perhaps, somehow, she could help him become a man..?

Chapter 51. Seduction

Crag was nervous as he approached Sis's container. So far every meeting between the two of them had ended in disaster. As he approached her container the door was open and amongst the foliage he could hear her voice singing the gentle, lilting words of John Barleycorn.

'Ah - she does has a woman's heart,' he thought to himself as he made his way into her jungle garden.

'Hi Sis,' he offered as he found her pruning a small palm.'I see you're trimming your bush.'

'You pathetic perv..' She spat back. 'Can't you go and play with yourself or better yet, chuck yourself over the side and give us all a break.'

Things clearly hadn't started well for Crag but he persisted.

'Sis, I know we haven't always seen eye to eye but I want to ask your advice about something.'

'If you want to know how to top yourself, there's the sea down there or you can douse yourself in diesel oil - I've always got a match.'

'No, seriously Sis, I need your help, I know I'm hopeless with women and I was sort of hoping you could help me. Maybe give me some advice? Tell me where I'm going wrong perhaps?'

'Well you're breathing for a start,' she retorted,' never a good idea with a moron like you.'

'I've got no confidence,' he blurted.' I know I put on this big show of being strong and in control but underneath I'm scared of doing the wrong thing. I don't know why I do it and it usually gets me in deep water'

'Basically you're an idiot and buffoon,' Sis answered,' and that's a difficult one to overcome but how do you suppose I can help?'

'Umm..Well, part of the problem is that I have never had..You know..Err..With a woman.'

'Why am I not surprised by that?' she mocked,'actually that's not strickly true is it? In your *mind* you've had loads of women, you've got the stains on your trousers to prove it.'

'Yes..But..But,'he stammered,' I don't want to go through life being half a man, I want to feel complete.

'Well, you may not act much like a man, but judging by that giant bulge in your trousers you seem to have all the right bits. That is a *very* big bulge. Just how big are you?'

'Please don't say that,' pleaded Crag,' it only makes it even bigger and then I can't stop myself from ....you know, having to have the trousers cleaned again.'

'Well lover boy, you've a problem, haven't you? You need to talk about it but you can't because then you get too excited and it's quickly all over.' She looked down at his crotch. 'Look at that bulge, it's like a giant tent - you bad boy,' and she gave it a quick swipe.

Suddenly Crag felt strangely in control. The swipe had been enough to take his mind off exploding but he was still featuring a massive erection.

'Now that's better', purred Sis, looking down at it, 'let's see what we can do about your virginity…'

Chapter 52. Sex

'Now don't forget, big-boy,' she purred,'tell me when you want another slap, cos it's fine with me,' and she knelt in front of him and roughly pulled his trousers down around his ankles.
'My - that *is* a *big* one,' she gasped as she studied it, inches from her face.
'Want another swipe yet?'
'No, no it's fine,' blurted Crag, 'it's fine.'
'Good, cos I want to have a *really* good look at it. You've got a beauty, I want to hold it,' and she held it in two hands, studying it's hot, hard, veiny surface.
'Want another slap yet?'
'No I'm still OK,' he croaked, looking down at what she was doing.
'Mmm, wonder what it tastes like,' she teased as she took it in her mouth, letting her lips slide down the shaft, eyes closed in concentration, further and further down.'Mmm tastes good,' she murmured as she came up for air and let it pop out of her mouth. 'Want another swipe?'
'Yes please - be quick,' he pleaded. She gave it a quick slap.
'How's that - better?'
'Yes, that's good.'
'OK it's my turn now,' as she pushed him back, straddled him and gently eased him into her, slowly letting it slide completely in. 'Don't forget... I can always take it out and... give it... another slap,' she gasped, unable to fully concentrate.'Just tell me...God you're *so big!* '
She started to ride him, slowly at first, then gathering momentum, her hands pressing down hard on his shoulders. He called out that he needed another slap but she didn't hear him and didn't care, it was becoming urgent as she felt herself losing control. She was riding him faster and faster. He couldn't stop himself as he cried out in a pained anguish as he exploded and jerked inside her, while she sobbed out loud in wave after wave of intense, excruciating pleasure as they came together.
She stayed astride him, holding him in, savouring the moment. Reaching down between her legs, she felt for his escaping semen which she slowly licked off her fingers.
'Mmm..nice,' she murmured,'not bad for a new boy - how are you feeling?'

Crag could only stare into her eyes and grunt something lost in translation. After years of self-doubt and fumbled embarrassment, Crag had finally lost his virginity....

Chapter 53. Plot

Crag had become insufferable after his sexual exploits with Sis. He walked around the ship with a constant smug beam on his face, haranguing anyone he could, talking slyly about *"knowing the ways of a woman"* and became even more of a bore than he'd been previously. Soon the rest of the group were ignoring him, much as they had before.

The ship, meanwhile, had taken them to Tangier, where they had spent several nights ashore, making sure they didn't repeat the mistakes of Dakar. Esmee in particular had been severely shaken by the back-street bar incident and stayed close to Omah and Sis, enjoying herself but keeping out of trouble. Crag's loss of his virginity failed to spark much interest in Esmee who was spending more time with Omah, dazzled by his card skills and, of course, his splendid lush moustache.

Sven could often be seen huddled, deep in conversation with the Steward. Over the time they'd been on the ship, they had developed, what appeared to be, a bond of mutual respect. In public Sven still resorted to scrawling on his writing board to say something but privately, most of the group knew he was capable of speech but they chose to collude with the pretence, thinking he had good reason for it, which he certainly did have. The diversion of having to write everything down, was a great help in avoiding difficult questions. Difficult questions; like who he really was. The reason being, he was an impostor. His long-held obsession with the story of the missing U-57 and the hours of research, spent in that warm museum reading-room in Hannover had resulted in a plot of staggering complexity. He had learnt dearly from his failed insurance scam and would not make silly mistakes again. By surrounding himself with *Kregsmarine* U-Boat war memorabilia and certification - some of it faked - he presented to the world, the perfect image of a devoted son of a highly decorated World War II submariner and naval hero. Only Sven knew the real truth, that under the bandages he was a failed fraudster from East Berlin whose unknown father ran away when he was a baby, leaving the family in grinding poverty.

As he pondered the next stage of the plan, the Steward announced his presence at the door.

'Ahem, we've taken food and diesel on board and we're ready to cast-off but we've got a problem. That idiot Crag suspects something. We've got to talk..

Chapter 54. Doubts

Sven rolled his eyes upwards. That idiot Crag was the bane of his life.
'What's he been saying now?' he snapped to the Steward,'I didn't think he had enough brains to wipe his own arse.'
'Apparently,' intoned the Steward,' he's been talking to Esmee and the others about a conspiracy on board.'
'What could he possibly know, said Sven,'the fool's always too busy fussing over his appearance to notice anything else.'
'Apparently he overheard you talking to the Old Bent Crone about the wartime accident and *Operation Quadriga*.
'So what? There's nothing he could possibly know about any of it. If that's all he's overheard, we don't have a problem.'
The Steward shifted uncomfortably. 'Maybe we should make sure he doesn't hear anymore, on a err..umm permanent basis.'
Sven looked at the Steward's expressionless face.'What are you saying? - that we should kill him?'
'I was thinking more about an unfortunate, ahem...accident.'
Sven looked again at the Steward and felt a chill run through him. The starched uniform, the blank expression and the cold, ice-blue eyes reminded him of a serial-killer he'd once seen in a waxworks museum and it scared him. Fraud was one thing, or even outright robbery, but not murder...Sven suddenly felt out of his depth and wondered if the Steward had been responsible for the three previous "accidents" on board the *Lagos Star*.
'No..No,'he said firmly,' there won't be any need for that. We all know the man's a complete fool. It's not necessary and he might even be useful in the future.'
For the first time, Sven had become doubtful. Thank goodness he hadn't told the Steward all of his plans. It was his guarantee of staying alive, but he knew from now on, he would have to start watching his back…

Chapter 55. Ginger

The ship's new co-ordinates had been programmed in. She had left Tangier and was sailing northwards off the Spanish coastline towards Cadiz. The departed Captain's cabin had been used for another meeting to decide their future course but the outcome had been muddled and undecided.

The feeling of mistrust, like an autumn chill, had found it's way into the group and was difficult to dispel. Where there had previously been a warm camaraderie - in part due to the shared group jeopardy - there was now a host of hidden agendas, none of which needed to be exposed or discussed, for fear of breaking fragile friendships. As a result, no specific destination had been agreed, just an agreement to head north to the next stop for supplies.

Crag, of course, was oblivious to these subtleties, being fully occupied with improving his own physical appearance. His moustache had grown back since the unfortunate explosion and was being constantly trimmed to maintain it's clipped perfection, as was his hair, which had developed a strange quirk.

After the explosion he had been left with only a few burnt tufts which had been shaved off and tidied up by Esmee. Initially Crag had been pleased his hair was regrowing and he was looking forward to trying some new elaborate coiffures, perhaps even contemplating elaborate comb-overs incorporating ear or nostril hair extensions to maximise the impact.

However he had been somewhat dismayed to find that his new hair had a definite gingerish quality to it. In fact, as time went on, it was becoming more and more ginger.

That in itself would have been difficult enough for Crag to come to terms with but the situation was being made worse by the fact that amongst the new luxuriant ginger growth, there were two streaks of white hair, like two comet streaks, each side of his forehead, sweeping back over his head, down to his neck which gave him a badger-like appearance and quickly earnt him the name of the Ginger Badger.

'Ah - here comes the Ginger Badger,' was a familiar taunt from Omah as Crag hurried past him and his small group of smirking onlookers.'Hurry back to your set, Ginger, before the Griffon sees you and fancies some lunch..ha..ha.'

'One day,' thought Crag,as he organised his wardrobe. 'One day we'll see who has the last laugh..'

So... as the days drifted past, each of the ship's inmates tried to avoid any future decisions and busied themselves with the minutiae of their own lives.

Paul the rock-star, spent his days in a fug of marijuana re-enacting his past days of glory, playing the guitar solos that once had rocked the Houston Astrodome and Madison Square Gardens, while Sven went over and over the documentation he had acquired from his years of research in the Hannover Museum reading room.

Omah spent his days perfecting new, more flamboyant card tricks. Sis worked through her exercise regime and tended her jungle garden while her sister Esmee danced and pirouetted around the decks, flirting with the men. During all this, the Old Bent Crone sat, rocking in her chair, letting the rosary beads slip through her bony fingers as she murmured soothing words to the Griffon, occasionally stroking it's cruppers...

Below decks, the uniformed Steward sat erect in his chair, stony faced, his ice-cold blue eyes staring back at him from the mirror, planning his next move...

Chapter 56. Ghostly Pipes

Two thousand miles north from where the *Lagos Star* was ploughing it's way through warm blue waters - on the uninhabited island rock of Thought in the outer reaches of the Western Isles, the weather was grim. Even by Western Isle standards the weather on Thought was known to be extra harsh due to its exposed position. Today, the wind howled mercilessly, driving rain horizontally against the black cliffs, where it ran down in torrents, back into the pitching heaving sea. The low leaden skies, barely skimming the top of the rock, were almost black in part, bringing the promise of more driving, incessant rain.

The island - situated between the islands of Sandray and Barra Head - was practically unapproachable by sea, with it's huge, black towering cliffs, heavy swell and barren, wind-blasted treeless landscape. The original small jetty had long ago been smashed to pieces by North Atlantic winter gales and nowadays the only way a landing could be achieved was by helicopter on the only flat surface available, a smallish courtyard, high in the ruined remains of the old monastery, long since abandoned.

Not that helicopter landings were easy. With the island being uninhabited and the winds treacherous, only the rarest visits occurred - even in the calm days of the summer months - usually just the briefest stops by Research Scientists to retrieve data and maintain the small weather station. The only other visitors to come near the island, apart from the hordes of nesting gulls and gannets were occasional amateur ornithologists, who arrived by locally chartered boat to monitor the gull numbers, staying well away from the vertical cliffs that rose up from the Atlantic swell and certainly not attempting to land.

The history of this forbidding rocky fortress had been passed down and embellished over the years. During the Dissolution of the Monasteries in the 14th.century, a group of Trappist monks had fled from persecution and with amazing belief and fortitude had built the monastery, living and surviving the harsh environment for over fifty years. Eventually they were beaten by malnutrition and disease - probably caused by the poor diet - which wiped out most of the community. The few remaining monks, believed to be just four in number, fled the rock, setting out for a settlement on Sandray. Unfortunately disease had left them weak, they weren't strong enough for the sea journey, bad weather capsized their boat and they were lost, their bodies washed ashore a week later.

The island of Thought stayed deserted until the 18th century, when the Scottish Laird, Hamish McKnuckie-Tavish (known locally as Mad Dog McKnuckie) bought the island and lived there alone, attempting repairs to the monastery and quietly going insane with the solitude. His remains were never found.

Local legend has it, that on cold winter nights, ye' can hear the pipes of Mad Dog practicing the refrain of *Cock O' The North*, as his ghost walks amongst the ruined walls...

"Ye' listening to the howling cry, it's no the wind you've caught.
That eerie wail that frightens thee, Och 'aye the Bagpipes of Thought…."

Chapter 57. Some DIY

Hamish McKnuckie-Tavish stepped from the small boat onto his personal island and bade the ferryman goodbye. Yes his very own island - his own soil - except there wasn't much of it on Thought..Not a lot of soil.. just rock...lot's of rock....more or less just rock...(certainly very rocky).. No matter he bravely thought(?) I can rebuild this pathetic excuse for a monastery. Just because it's now only the 18th century, that doesn't stop me, single handedly, on a hostile rocky outcrop, restoring this 14th former monastery, which is now a complete ruin.

And so the sad, sorry decline of Hamish McKnuckie-Tavish (aka. Mad Dog McKnuckie) started it's gruesome journey as he opened his first packet of mortar and cursed himself for forgetting a trowel. But his few possessions; a spare tartan, a book of collected *Rabbie Burns* and of course his trusty bagpipes - complete with spare reed - was all he'd ever needed. He'd arrived home....

Chapter 58. Defeat

For the next few weeks, Hamish -Mad Dog- McKnuckie threw himself into the restoration work. He first constructed a rough shelter in the ruins of the old monastery kitchen. This small square room , now roofless, which originally had failed spectacularly to keep the monks fed, now also failed to successfully shelter Mad Dog from the howling winds but the dry stones were more or less intact. He strung a loose canvas tarpaulin across the tops of the kitchen's ruined walls and held it in place with twine and rocks. It flapped continuously but it kept off most of the driving rain.

In the evenings, with his strength sapped by hunger and the incessant cold, he sat huddled in a corner, wrapped in his spare tartan, practising his pipes until he fell asleep. Often a storm would blow in across the Atlantic in the early hours before light, roughly waking him - wretched and shivering - and he would once again take comfort from his bagpipes, playing again and again the *Cock O' the North* in a effort to defeat the roar of the wind.

As the days passed he became weaker. His dry rations were running low, he had seriously underestimated the work necessary and his own ability to survive the continuous wet and cold but the real problem was the island itself. It didn't want him there. It wanted to regain its solitude with just the company of the wind, rain and seabirds. Human beings didn't belong and weren't wanted on Thought.

In his last few weeks, Mad Dog gave up working on the ruins. His dry rations were finished and he'd been reduced to eating scraps of seaweed thrown up by the sea, or the odd dead seabird found amongst the rocks. He had no fire and was always cold. He tried to keep warm by routinely scrambling across the rocks, often falling and cutting himself in the process. His wounds weren't healing properly and he often thought he could hear voices carried to him on the wind. He was sure he could hear his mother urging him to hurry up for school or there were other times when he heard his sister crying because he'd been pulling her hair and mercilessly teasing her.

It was two months before the weather cleared sufficiently to allow a boat to land on the island. Three men in a fishing smack from Barra managed to get a line secured in the calm swell and scrambled up the rocks to the ruins. They found the remains of the canvas tarpaulin, now reduced to shreds, a few empty tins and his beloved bagpipes - carefully stored in a dry corner - but no sign of Mad Dog McKnuckie. They split up and scoured the island but there was no trace - he'd simply disappeared. As they made their way cautiously back down to their boat the conversation was sombre. The assumption was made that he had slipped whilst foraging for food and drowned. A better assumption to make, than to think of a man, driven insane by his own loneliness and starvation, throwing himself sixty feet onto the jagged, foam covered rocks below.

As the small crew made ready and began to push away from the rock, they suddenly stopped what they were doing, looked askance at each other as they distinctly heard *Cock O' the North*, being played expertly by the Bagpipes of Thought

Chapter 59. Legend

The men standing in the fishing smack were made of the strongest stuff. They were Hebridean fishing stock - used to everything the North Atlantic storms could throw at them. Their fathers had been fishermen, their fathers before them. They had more salt water in their veins than blood. They looked at each other, speechless, as the sound of the pipes drifted down to where they bobbed in the light swell.

'Should we na' go back and take a second look?' one of them offered.

The skipper of the boat was apprehensive..'The weather will be coming in soon, we'll nae' want to be caught out here.'

Calum Fraser, the third and youngest was keen to check,'It'll nae take me long, give me five minutes,' and he jumped off the boat and scrambled up the rock face.

What he saw when he rounded the top of the cliff and looked into the ruined shelter made the blood drain from his face. He stood stock still, not believing what he was seeing...The bagpipes were still where they had last seen them, stowed in a corner but - *they were playing themselves*. They were being animated by unseen hands with the refrain of *Cock O' the North* issuing forth. Calum stood rooted to the spot, unable to move, staring in terrified disbelief.

His frozen stance was eventually broken by shouts from below..'C'mon son, the weather's coming in fast, we have to leave.. NOW!'

He half scrambled, half fell back down the cliff to the waiting boat and leaped on board as they pushed off and set sail for Barra. Clouds were driving in from the west and the wind had picked up. They cranked the mainsail tight against the wind and felt the familiar surge as the wooden boat creaked and lurched into the choppy waves, picking up a good speed, anxious to be in safe harbour.

Not much was said on the journey back, all three men were trying to come to terms with what they'd seen and heard. Especially Calum who sat, white faced and shivering as the others busied themselves with navigation. It was only later that evening, when they were safely back on Barra, sitting in the snug, smokey comfort of the Castlebay bar that they tried to make sense of what had happened to them on the island. Crusty, pipe smoking patrons in the bar crowded round, better to hear the story, anxious not to miss any of the details. Calum was pleased to find that he didn't have to buy a drink for the next three months, but it didn't compensate for not being able to sleep through the nights, his fitful dreams interrupted by the sound of those eerie pipes.

Not a week went passed without it being discussed by the Barra community. Over the years the Legend of the Bagpipes of Thought was kept alive by successive locals and fishermen. Calum's family were especially proud of their connection to the story - much loved by tourists - and to this day, hanging over the hotel bar in pride of place, is a framed and faded sepia photo of Calum Fraser with his two old friends, standing by their fishing boat, smiling for the camera, readying to set sail... Much as they had done, on that strange, unforgettable day to Thought - all those years ago…

Chapter 60. Banter

Two thousand miles away to the south, the *Lagos Star* ploughed relentlessly on, passing the St Vincent Point lighthouse off the Portuguese coast, heading northwards. The clear azure sea was mirror calm with the sky an unbroken blue as Esmee frolicked out on deck, dressed in a near transparent sun-dress and a pair of easily identified skimpy pants.

Eventually she stopped twirling and dancing and lay back, exhausted on a deck chair. Sitting next to her, Omah picked up some cards and started shuffling.

'Oh my dearest,' he complained, 'why did you stop, I was just enjoying it, especially watching the sun through your dress.'

'Oh Omah,' she trilled,' you are such a *rude* man, I can see I'm going to have to take you in hand.'

'Oh I do hope so my dear,' he drawled,' I can't wait, just tell me when, I'll be ready and waiting.'

'It looks like you're already ready,' she guffawed looking down pointedly at his shorts, ' either that or you've brought a torch with you. Expecting a power-cut are we?'

'Well you know what they say in the Scouts,' he replied, ' always be prepared eh?'

'Mmm.. I didn't know they had Boy Scouts in Cairo,' she admonished, wagging her finger,' I thought they used boys for other activities there - what is it they say?..''*a woman for fun but a boy for pleasure?*''

Omah bridled at the accusation, 'I wouldn't know about that, perhaps you're confusing my honourable birthplace with somewhere else in the Med.'

'Perhaps I am,' she opined, getting bored,' so very sorry if the great Omah's upset.' She pulled down her large-brimmed sun hat, effectively finishing the conversation.

The awkward silence was broken by the chinking of ice in glasses as Crag made an appearance by their sides, carrying some drinks.

'Ahh, it's the Ginger Buffoon, aka Batman's Robin' sneered Omah,'how thoughtful of you. I just feel like a drink.'

'Get your own,' growled Crag,'these are for me and Esmee.'

Esmee tried hard to suppress a giggle. Crag had made a big effort to dress for the occasion but the effect was bizarre. His sandals, picked up in a street market in Tangier were the classic Moorish design with the toes pointed up and curling in a semi-circle but unfortunately they were not designed to be worn with grey M&S calf length socks. Also the enormous shorts that Crag had chosen from his Man-On-Safari collection had more to do with the late Eric Morecombe than Daktari. The safari shirt, with it's many pockets and epaulets was several sizes too small, giving him an odd onion shape, like a rogue member from the *"Garden Gang"* books. All this topped off with a tightly clipped moustache and the ginger and white streaked hair was too much for Esmee who tilted her hat further down but could not stop her shoulders shaking as she started to giggle uncontrollably.

Undeterred, Crag sat down and started to load his trusty pipe with the rough shag obtained by the lackey in Dakar, making a mental note to himself to wire ahead to his trusted friend off the Burlington Arcade for new supplies.

'You look ridiculous,' mumbled Omah as Esmee nearly fell out of her deck-chair with uncontrolled hysteria.

Crag - pretending not to hear - clenched hard down on his pipe and thrust his lantern jaw out towards the blue horizon....

Chapter 61. Stewart Steward

Below decks, Stewart the Steward brooded alone in his cabin. Things had not gone well with Sven or the Old Bent Crone. He needed to be sure of them if things were going to work according to plan. He prided himself on being a good judge of people and had probed until he had found Sven's weaknesses; his love of money and his hopeless insecurity. The Old Bent Crone was a different story, harder to fathom, an enigma. She apparently had a much more serious objective - revenge - and seemed to be prepared to wait until she could serve it up, at its best temperature - ice cold.

As he ironed and starched his white uniform, he was feeling annoyed and cheated. He'd spent most of his adult life thinking of - and serving - others. After leaving the Army catering corp he'd had a succession of jobs, mostly on cruise ships or private yachts. He'd graduated to a brief spell on the Royal Yacht Britannia until that unfortunate episode with the young, good looking radio-officer. The Palace could not cope with another scandal and so he had been unceremoniously dumped at Gibraltar with a few hundred pounds and told to keep his mouth shut - or else.

In desperation, he'd tried to get some hotel work along the Spanish Costas but failed to impress or match the energy of the locals and had eventually hitched into France, gravitating to the port of Marseille. His schoolboy French was enough to get him agency work on merchantmen and container ships from where he'd drifted into the pay of the Serbian company, where no questions were ever asked and to his present position on the *Lagos Star*. The title of Steward was a fictitious affectation on his part. He had been hired as cook and general help. The elevated position was of his own invention, the uniform bought secondhand, from a theatrical costumier. His cold, expressionless face stared back at him from the mirror. Had he not helped these people through some difficult times? Had he not been courteous and helpful? He'd been on hand, serving them with drinks and food, organising parties, helping them with their laundry. And what he received in return? - He was taken for granted, treated like a skivvy and most importantly he'd not been included in any of their plans. Sure Sven had shared some information with him, but he'd not had to get *his* hands dirty. It was Steward who had helped solve the problem of the Anglo-Swedish industrialist and the disgraced English MP, both of whom had seen fit to want a share in the potential good fortune, whilst contributing nothing.

They both deserved what had happened to them. It was a shame the Captain had to go - Steward had liked him - but he'd become obstructive. In the way. Insisting the ship had to keep to its schedule. Luckily the ship practically sailed itself, making the Captain superfluous to requirements. The Steward pondered his next move. He was beginning to think that the bandaged Sven had outlived his usefulness…

Chapter 62. 1943

It was the height of World War II and the tide was turning against the Nazis and Adolf Hitler. His armies were becoming stretched on all fronts, in the north African desert, in the Russian winter after the disaster of Stalingrad, and in northern France. The factories in the Ruhr were working to full capacity, churning out trucks, planes and munitions but these resources were insufficient for a war out of control, on multiple fronts. Unfortunately Hitler, with his insane, twisted obsession for the construction of more and more death-camps failed to realise he should have used the materials and labour for the construction of war-machine factories. What the Nazis needed was another source of weaponry, another source of armaments if they were to overcome their enemies.

To the north sat the country of Sweden. It had its own well equipped army and comprehensive navy but had declared itself neutral at the outset of war and had therefore been left alone. It was however becoming a very poor country, it's trade routes were effectively blocked, it's people were being denied business abroad and the Swedish State Treasury was becoming depleted.

During one of the fraught meetings at the *Wolf's Lair* at Rastenburg, less than a year before the assassination attempt on his life, Hitler, attended by his nervous Generals were discussing an idea. They would send a secret emissary to Stockholm with a proposition. A proposition that would help both countries. The Nazi emissary would secretly negotiate a significant purchase of Swedish armaments and munitions in exchange for the most sought after, anonymous and discrete currency of them all; Gold. Whether it was Swiss, Nazi or American, it was all the same, especially after the smelting process. The *Bundesbanke* was broke - the war had seen to that - but Hitler, with his studies of the evolution of the Third Reich from it's Prussian beginnings, thought he knew exactly where to find it.

One of the most famous landmarks in Germany, is the Brandenburg Gate in Berlin. It has straddled the city for more than three centuries, as a symbol of Prussian power. On top of the columns sits the Quadriga statue of Victory, the Roman goddess of war, astride her war-chariot, pulled by four powerful stallions. When Napoleon's armies beat Prussia in 1806 he had it dismantled and taken back to Paris, as part of his victory spoils. Eight years later, when the Prussian army beat France, the Quadriga was recaptured and restored to it's original position on the Brandenburg Gate. On the original sculpture, the goddess Victory held aloft a staff with a spread eagle and the symbol of peace - a wreath of olive leaves. When the statue was returned to Germany, the spread eagle was enlarged and the wreath was replaced by the Iron Cross, the acknowledged symbol of Prussian might.

In an ostentatious show of wealth, it was decreed in 1814, by King Fredricke William III that all the four new pieces of the statue including the spread eagle, the iron cross emblem and the cross shaped staff were to be cast in solid gold. These new additions stood at over two metres in height, one and a half meters wide and collectively weighed in at over a ton.

Over a century later, on a freezing wet Berlin night in March 1943, six *Gestapo* workmen with ropes and pulleys were surreptitiously hoisted onto the top of the Brandenburg Gate in near darkness, where they started to dismantle the precious sections and replace them with gilt replicas. By the next morning, their work had been done. Observed from the ground, the Brandenburg Gate and Quadriga looked the same as usual - proud and defiant in the day's cold sunlight - but Hitler now had his precious blood money and would soon have his weapons…

Chapter 63. Hope

It may have been a night to remember for Crag but for Big Sis it was definitely a night to forget. She had finally relented to Crag's constant demands for more sexual tuition despite her own misgivings. The truth was, he was easy and she still had her own needs to consider. She had no intention or desire to develop a relationship with him - she still thought of him as a buffoon and fool - but the sex had been OK and there weren't that many men on the ship to choose from. She actively disliked the oily Omah and Paul the ex-rock-star always seemed to be on another hazy, far away planet (plus she doubted his ability to perform) and she found the Steward just too downright creepy. That only left Crag and Sven. She liked Sven, she felt he was probably a kind person but how could she really tell? Who or what was behind those bandages? Conversation was difficult with him at best; either muffled mumbles or the writing board, neither method of communication suggesting nights of unbroken passion. And then of course *that* face. What was it *really* like under all that tightly wound cotton? Supposing it was hideously deformed ?...Sweating, inches away, from hers ? ..She'd have to look away ugh! No - the risk was too great, it was Crag the buffoon or nothing.

The evening had started quite well. Sis had made an effort, wearing her finest and most alluring loincloth and her tattoos were looking their best. She had made her speciality dish: fish caught over the side and a jungle salad made with shoots & leaves from her container garden.The meal was finished off with several steaming cups of good strong cruppers tea.

As Sis started to clear away the plates, Crag cleared his throat...

'Well then m'gal, how's about some of that slap and tickle eh?'

She gave him a withering look.'Is that the best you can up with? Is that your best chat up line? You've sat there all night, deep in thought, I was imagining something more inspiring.'

'Sorry old girl,' he blurted,' I was thinking about my new hairstyle.'

Big Sis rolled her eyes upwards. 'You really are priceless, have you never heard of seduction?'

'Oh yes that. Isn't that just in the movies?'

'No it's not you idiot, it's what couples do with each other in real life. It makes for excitement, for some real *j'oi de vivre*.'

Hmm, not that keen on French food myself - I find it too greasy,' as he reached for his trusty pipe.

This was all too much for Sis.

'I'll tell you what!' she exclaimed, half-shouting, 'why don't you bugger off, back to your own container and work out something original to say and maybe, just maybe, I'll let you back in here sometime. Until then go and think about your ridiculous, bloody, self-absorbed self!'

With that she picked him up bodily by his Man-on-Safari shirt and threw him out the door.

As he picked himself up from the steel deck, brushing off some flecks of rust from his trousers he gazed thoughtfully into the clear, starry, night sky. 'Hmm, playing hard to get eh...?'

Back in her container Sis sat annoyed and frustrated, deciding Crag was permanently beyond help. Perhaps she'd been too dismissive of Sven ....?

Chapter 64. The Blues

The noise of sustained guitar feedback coming from ex-rock star Paul's container was frightening and yet magnificent. From the bows to the stern of the *Lagos Star*, the distorted, tortured, sustained D chord from a Stratocaster could be heard echoing out across the waves. Outside Paul's container the sound was deafening - inside it was surgical.

Three 100w Marshall stacks wired in series. 24 twelve inch speakers being overdriven with the volume turned to eleven. What was he thinking of? What Paul was thinking of - was oblivion.

He'd had another troubled nights sleep. The memories of past glories had kept returning; brief snatches of his on-stage fame, the time he opened for the Stones at Nice, the solo he played at Earls Court during the Blues

Beyond tour. All fantastic achievements but all in the past. What had he done lately?

After the fame and fortune he'd retired to the lazy LA sun, where his wife had soon become bored with him and left. In an effort to relive earlier, happier days, he'd formed other bands with some of his old music mates but without success. The spark had gone, he had peaked years ago. He realised his playing had now become a stale, cliche ridden joke.

He had been awake since the early dawn smoking too many of his 'jazz woodbines', trying to shake off the heavy miasma but without success. In fact his mood had deepened during the day to a point where even playing his guitar now seemed pointless. He kept smoking more until he found he'd lost the major use of his limbs. He slumped lower into his chair, his head lolling back, guitar draped across his knees with the volume turned right up. Yes he thought,*"Death By Sound"* - he didn't care anymore, a good way to go.

He could feel the build up of blood in his temples. Any minute now, the vessels would haemorrhage and he would be bleeding from the ears, after which, total blackness as the blood leaked through to the brain's frontal lobes. Then that perfect silence...

Deep in his subconscious he heard the clang of metal, a metal door opening and then being roughly pulled up, his guitar falling to the floor…

Chapter 65. Friends

At first he thought he'd crossed over to the other side and was in heaven. There was a dazzling white light in his eyes and an angel looking down on him with a beautiful soft benevolence.

He soon realised he wasn't however, when a bucket of cold water hit him full in the face.

'What the *HELL* were you trying to do?!'

It was Sis leaning over him, shaking his shoulders, 'I came to tell you about the noise; you'd passed out, what on earth were you playing at?'

'I...I'm sorry, 'he blurted, 'It was stupid of me, I'm so sorry..but thanks for rescuing me. I'm OK now.'

Sis was concerned. ' C'mon, walk with me round the deck, get some oxygen in you, you look terrible,' she lifted him up and supported him, as he stumbled along gasping for some fresh air.

Later on, as he sat in Sis's container, she busied herself making some strong cruppers tea.

'I've never been in here before,' he said,' this micro-jungle is amazing, how do you get it to grow?'

'Pure skill on my part,'she laughed,'I learned about jungle plants in Cambodia. I like to nurture them; watch them grow, some of them taste good too - very healthy, you should try it.'

'Yeah I guess I should eat better, just lately I haven't bothered.'

Sis looked directly at him with a steady gaze. 'We've never *really* talked have we? You've always seemed so...well, preoccupied with other things. It felt like I would be intruding.'

'Strange isn't it,' said Paul,' I've never felt as if I should talk to you either. You always seem so self-reliant, tough and strong. I thought if I started talking to you... you'd well, think I was coming on to you.'

Sis looked at him again,' well you have got a bit of a reputation in that department, but I'm sure it's nothing I can't handle. I can always put you in your place can't I ?' and she laughed as she poured out the tea.

They sat and looked at each other fondly - in a new light. Paul was the first to speak.

'Thanks Sis - for everything.'

'Let's raise a cup "to new horizons!"' she toasted as they both slurped the perfectly brewed tea.

'Hmm those cruppers make all the difference,' she murmured to herself...

Chapter 66. Face

Sven was, at last, comfortable within himself. As he stood at the ship's rail, looking out at the azure sea, he'd reached a major conclusion. He'd decided to come out. Not in a gay way - he wasn't of that persuasion - but to strip off the head and face bandages that had blighted his life for so long and to accept the consequences.

There were two problems he had to come to terms with: Firstly his appearance. The botched plastic surgery was still in evidence, his slack face looking like an advanced stroke victim, with one eye semi-shut and his mouth sagging to one side. On refection, looking at it from a casual observer's perspective, it probably wasn't *that* bad, but Sven knew it wasn't *his* face, not the face he had started out with. He would have to get used to it. It would certainly look better once it was exposed to the sun and fresh air. At the moment perpetually covered up, it had a ghostly look of a cadaver.

The second problem he faced was the identity issue: He was here on the *Lagos Star* posing as the son of a World War II hero, the captain of U-57. Without the bandages he was sure he'd be discovered as a fraud and imposter ... but why?

As far as he knew there were only a handful of old grainy photos depicting the great man amongst the memorabilia and none of the son. In fact he couldn't be sure if the captain even *had* a son, there'd been no record of one during the extensive research. These thoughts put Sven's mind at ease and he decided to bite the bullet that night and remove the bandages, showing his new, strange face to the group and world for the first time.

As he gazed out to sea, he was so pleased and relieved with his decision, he failed to notice the shadowy figure in the starched white suit creeping towards him. The first he knew of another's presence was when he felt a sharp tug as he was lifted up bodily by his legs and jacket collar. He was being hoisted over the rail... he was powerless, his flailing hands could only clutch at the empty air …

Chapter 67. Saved

As Sven prepared to meet his maker, a strange thing happened. Instead of being pitched forward into the sea, he found himself propelled backwards where he landed on something soft, something human - the Steward. Standing over them both was Big Sis.

'OK start talking ,' she declared, speaking to the Steward, one of her feet holding him down,' I saw it all, what's your game eh?'

Sven rolled away from the prone, defeated Steward and stood up. Now was as good time as any, he started to unwind the bandages from his neck and face in front of Sis.

'My God!' she exclaimed, ' first I uncover a killer in our midst and now *"The Return of the Mummy"* uncovers himself. I need to sit down.'

'Sis you haff my undying gratitude,' said Sven,' you saved my life from this...this monster.'

The Steward was saying nothing, staring expressionless into the middle distance.

Sis looked at Sven's revealed face with interest. She'd seen many disfigurements during her time cage-fighting in Cambodia, many much worse than Sven's. She was intrigued.

'I thought you had massive burns and scars or something,' she said,' why do you keep the bandages on?'

'I'm embarrassed and it's a long story,' he muttered, looking away, avoiding her eyes, ' I vill tell you tonight if you are interested?'

'OK but first we have to decide what to do with this pathetic psycho. I think we can assume he also murdered the Captain, the Anglo-Swedish industrialist and the English MP. We'd be perfectly entitled to throw *him* over the side to sleep with the fishes.'

'I didn't kill the industrialist,' mumbled the Steward,' I didn't have anything to do with that one.'

'Hmm, whether you did or not, no one will believe you anyway,' said Sis,' we'll put you in one of the storage lockers for now,' and she pulled him up and dragged him down to the storage areas below decks.

As she slammed the door and slid the bolt home to Steward's prison, her mind was churning over the recent events. This had certainly been a day to remember, she was looking forward to telling the others. She strolled purposefully round to Esmee's container to tell her the news, her tattoos rippling in the hot sun..

Chapter 68. Soiree

That night, Big Sis invited everyone round to her container to an "Eats Shoots & Leaves" party and to bring everybody up to date on recent developments. She had spent the day picking only the most tender and succulent foliage from her micro-jungle, delicately infusing them with only the finest herbs and spices. She gently simmered the food, wrapped in elephant bark, on the top of a small clay oven.

She'd had the oven installed while they were in Tangier by a local artisan. A small, wiry, Moorish gentleman had brought it to the ship on her instructions, his back, bent double with the weight. When she'd shown him her tattoos, he'd laughed out loud, revealing a solitary, tobacco stained tooth.

Inside the oven she had some previously prepared, freshly caught fish, couched in *whaarno* leaves with a *nagaali* and cruppers garnish which was gently awaiting her guest's greedy mouths.

First to arrive was ex-rock star Paul. Sis had asked him to bring his acoustic guitar - she loved to hear him play - and he sat on an old pouffe, gently picking out the refrain from a traditional Andalusian love-song. The more she found out about this man, the more intrigued she became.

Slowly the rest of the group arrived and were welcomed with glasses of juice from berries of the *cack-cack* bush. Esmee arrived looking radiant in an off the shoulder number made of lace and taffeta, her fair beauty shining with an inner luminescence. Crag followed meekly behind, his blue safari suit crumpled and stained without the Stewards attentions. He'd attempted to revive his ginger streaked hair ensemble with the popular gelled look. Unfortunately the absence of gel on the ship had forced him to improvise with ship's grease, the pervasive aroma of animal by-products resulting in a two metre Crag exclusion zone. Next to arrive was Omah, looking cool and svelt in a white tuxedo with red cummerbund. His moustache was outstanding - truly magnificent. Crag could only gasp in admiration.

Sis had briefed the others about the new bandage-less Sven but it was still a shock when he arrived, which they all did their best to disguise. It was shocking, but not in a horrific or grotesque way, but because it was like seeing a new strange person they'd never encountered before. They'd been used to seeing Sven's head completely plaster wrapped and covered and here it was ...well fairly *ordinary*. The men all shook his hand, with Esmee and Sis kissing him lightly on his cheek, which made him shy and embarrassed. He turned away and looked for something to concentrate on.

Last to arrive was the Old Bent Crone, complete with the Griffon vulture perched on her arm, it's fierce unblinking eyes looking for prey...

Chapter 69. Gloomy

Crag pulled nervously at the sub-standard creases of his Man-on-Safari pale blue trousers.

The evening party had gone well and now most of the group had left Sis's party and returned to their own lives. The Old Bent Crone had been the first to leave (the Griffon had been playing up) - followed by Sven, who had been mightily relieved his face hadn't frightened anyone.

The mood in the container was mellow; Sis was sitting close next to Paul, stroking his hair, as he played a gentle Spanish lullaby. Esmee was snuggled up to Omah, both of them giggling as he showed her some new card tricks.

Crag busied himself loading his pipe with extreme concentration, anxious to show he hadn't noticed the intimate atmosphere. He clenched the pipe tightly between his teeth, thrusting his lantern-jaw towards the direction of Paul's guitar, trying to loose himself in the Spanish rhythms and pretending not to notice the intimate signs of affection being shown by the two couples.

Eventually Omah was the first to speak. 'I say old man, ever feel like a spare part?'

Crag blustered, ' Err oh yes must be going soon, have some ironing to take care of eh?'

'Don't let us stop you then,' drawled Omah,' goodnight old boy.'

Crag stood up and mumbled a goodnight to everyone and left. As he walked away from the container he heard the sound of laughing behind him and felt wretched. The two women that had become his mainstay were enjoying themselves and didn't need him around. He opened the door to his container and looked around at the familiar objects, placed exactly where he'd last left them. The clothes draped untidily over chairs. The Mr Suave manicure wallet still sat next to the make-up mirror. The bottle of hair-dye had spilt and was staining the sink and the pile of dirty dishes had settled deep into their own ooze.

He rinsed off a dirty cup and poured himself three fingers of 25yr old *Cahtspiece* malt, chased by an astringent Bulgarian Cava and pondered his next move. Maybe he should quit the ship at the next port of call, there was nothing for him here…

Chapter 70. The Plan

The evening was a great success with everyone complimenting Sis on a terrific meal and great company. As the fake Titanic printed plates (found in one of the containers) were cleared away, it was time to discuss the future.

Sven was the first to speak. 'Friends - I believe I can call you my friends after what has happened on this journey' ..He swallowed and continued, ' I'm here on a false pretence. I'm not the son of a highly decorated U-Boat captain but a fraudster from East Berlin who tried to defraud an insurance company with a false identity and that's why my face carries the unnatural look of a botched plastic surgery. During my time in isolation after the surgery, I spent many days in libraries out of boredom and became interested and researched a story from World War II concerning a U-Boat, U-57 to be exact which was rumoured to have gone missing carrying a large consignment of Nazi gold to Sweden to help buy arms for Hitler's war effort.'

'Neither the U-Boat or the gold ever reached Sweden. Many stories have circulated around this mystery. Some say the crew hijacked the vessel took it to the Republic of Ireland, where they shared out the gold and either used it to get to South America after the war or simply melted into Irish life and became citizens. This is quite possible as at the end of the war, the huge fleet of surrendered U-Boats were corralled off the Irish coast where they were moored up and later towed out to sea and used as target practice by the Royal Navy. However that particular U-57 was never recorded as being surrendered so is there a possibility it was lost en-route to Ireland with it's precious cargo? The navigation route would have taken the vessel over Scotland's northern tip, down the Western Isles into the Irish Sea where there are many instances of ships lost on the treacherous rocky coast off Barra Head during the Atlantic winter storms. Earlier surveys carried out in the 1970s revealed several wrecks including one cigar shaped wreck on the sea bed about the size of a submarine. It could be the U-57...'

Chapter 71. Greed

The silence in Sis's jungle container was deafening as they all tried to take it all in.

Omah broke the silence. 'So what about the Industrialist, the MP, the Steward, the Captain?'

'They were all involved in the plan' continued Sven ' the Industrialist had the necessary funds and contacts to hire this ship. The heavy lifting gear, sonar and undersea scanning equipment is all secreted in various containers here on board. He paid for it all. Who would suspect a normal well used container ship just going around the oceans with its cargo of anonymous boxes?'

'The MP had connections. Connections that gave us maritime survey licences and salvage and territorial marine rights and ensured we were not questioned too closely. The Steward isn't a steward at all. He's a fixer and he learnt to deep sea dive when he worked on boats out of Marsielles. His time on the Royal Yacht was useful too. The Captain was a captain of sorts - he had a Captain's Certificate issued by the Somali authorities after the necessary "brown envelopes" were exchanged during the ship repairs'.

'So what happened?' said Sis.

'GREED' replied Sven.'it's always greed.. We couldn't agree on the individual shares between us should we get lucky and the Steward took it on himself to reduce the number of participants. I wouldn't be here either had it not been for you Sis - thank you for saving my life'.

'What happens now?' Paul was mildly curious and was wondering if he could work it into a song..

'I don't know' said Sven. 'I really don't know'...

Chapter 72. Old Bent Crone

The Old Bent Crone was confused. She'd been confused for a while now, ever since she was on her 'once in a lifetime' Caribbean cruise. She had enjoyed taking in the food and entertainment on board the *Sapphire Princess,* a huge white monolithic monstrosity that looked more like a floating block of ugly flats - the kind often seen from a taxi en route from an airport - than an ocean going ship.

It was the sightseeing stop at Antigua when things went badly wrong. She had disembarked with most of the other cruise passengers at St Johns dockside where they were told they had a free afternoon to explore the sights the Antiguan capital had to offer.

In truth there wasn't too much to explore. After 15 minutes she'd seen most of the town and needed to find somewhere to sit away from the afternoon's heat. She found herself in a brightly painted but fairly shabby open bar frequented by locals who regarded her with interest. She ordered a local beer , even though she wasn't a beer drinker and soon found herself absorbed with the local culture including a young man with a brightly coloured parrot on his arm.

The parrot was chattering away in a quasi English accent which fascinated the Old Crone.

"I sell you this parrot, he will be your best friend" said the young man ' very cheap for you".

'I love him but I can't ' she said, ' I'm on the cruise ship and leaving in an hour or so'.

" No worries" said the young man. ' He comes with a cage so very safe and they will allow him on board definitely'.

The Old Bent Crone was not convinced but was keen to have company on board ship.

They arranged to meet on the dockside later, when money would be exchanged and she would be the proud owner of a chatty, brightly coloured parrot in a cage. She sat relaxed and had another beer or two..

Later, as the Old Bent Crone waited on the dockside she began to worry about this unlikely transaction when the young man arrived with the caged bird.

It was only after the money had changed hands and the young man had quickly disappeared that she noticed the bird seemed somehow different from the last time she saw it back in the bar- it seemed bigger and was definitely less chatty. Her confusion was interrupted by the blast from the ship's discordant whistle hurrying the last few tourists back on board. In her distracted state, she dashed up the gangplank with the bird.

She was surprised there wasn't the usual smartly dressed steward to meet and greet her on board. She was even more surprised when she looked and saw her *Sapphire Princess* slowly ease her bulk away from the mooring next door...the Old Bent Crone had got on the wrong ship! Before she could see or contact anyone, she was horrified to feel that this ship was moving too. She looked around at the rusty deck and the shabby containers. She was trapped. The bird in the cage fixed her with a stare and remained silent..

Worse was to come. Before she had a chance to find shelter, a typical Caribbean afternoon tropical rainstorm arrived, quickly soaking her to the skin. She then watched aghast as the bright jungle colours of her new bird were getting washed out by the rain, dripping from the feathers revealing a dull brown and grey but proud and defiant bird of prey. Not only was the Crone trapped on a rust-bucket container ship, she had purchased a new unwelcome companion, a Griffon vulture....

Chapter 73. Decision

The *Lagos Star* ploughed its way northwards as the weather deteriorated , through the Irish Sea and out into the open Atlantic on its way to the Western Isles.

A decision had been reached - by a small majority- that the group would pursue the journey to the end and maybe, just maybe they would be able to salvage the gold from the U-57 lying on the sea bed south of Barra Head. Money and provisions were running low and Omah, Sis, Sven and Paul saw it as route to regain status and new beginnings. Esmee didn't like the rough weather: Crag agreed and was also concerned about how the journey was affecting his Man on Safari wardrobe collection so voted with Esmee against and the Old Bent Crone was just confused..

As the old ship pitched and rolled in the open Atlantic it was becoming increasingly clear that they would need some help when they arrived at the wreck site. In the meantime they would sail on to Barra and anchor in the relative calm of Castlebay to the south of the island and perhaps be able to enlist some local help from fishermen with the dive and recovery.

Eventually- after a day of howling gale and horizontal rain and stinging spray, the GPS steered the *Lagos Star* into the relative calm of Barra's Castlebay where they dropped anchor a distance off-shore. They managed to launch the small tender boat which doubled as an escape boat and chugged up to the small mooring jetty which served the tiny community of Castlebay. To the casual onlooker, as the group struggled the short distance up the street to the Castlebay Hotel they must have presented a strange picture. The tableau had an ageing rock-star in stage gear and a ridiculously dressed man in a crumpled safari suit. A flighty woman dressed more for a cocktail party accompanied by a man dressed for a night at the casino tables and an old woman with a Griffon vulture which was looking restless and ready to pounce. Only Sven in his overalls looked like he didn't belong in this weird fancy dress carnival. It was also the first time they had walked on dry land for many weeks and they found it an unsteady experience. A truly bizarre procession as the Barra locals stood and looked on baffled…

Chapter 74. Barra

That evening they all sat in the cozy bar of the Castlebay Hotel, listening to some of the favourite songs from the Nuremberg rallies. Sung by a quartet of fishermen dressed in oilskins, Crag had an eyrie feeling of deja vu. He recalled an earlier episode many months ago sat in a similar pub bar and hearing the same refrains. Perhaps just a coincidence?

He looked at the old framed sepia photos over the fireplace of past fishermen. Worthy brave men of the past who fought the cruel sea and sometimes lost. His eye was particularly drawn to a photograph of a a young beaming face of a tough looking lad - probably a fisherman dressed in oilskins with the name Calum Frazer written on the photo in pen.

"I say my man!" demanded Crag to the Barman, "I'd like to speak to this Calum chap" he said pointing at the picture.

" Aye you could try" answered the barman, " you'll not get much out of him. He's buried in the churchyard since 1948, he's not spoken to anyone since".

The others chortled and rolled eyes at each other. That Crag, always getting himself in embarrassing situations.

"But you could try his Grandson Young Calum, he's over there in the corner with the Nuremberg quartet, the one with the Scottish One String fiddle."

Crag smoothed down the creases in his Man on Safari suit and sidled over to the players and politely tapped his foot to one of their stirring marches. When they had finished he broached the subject of the photo.

"Aye that'll be my Grand daddy" said Callum Junior 'whose asking?'

'I've read about him ', said Crag 'I've read about him and the Legend, the Legend that belongs to the Island of Thought'.

At those words the bar froze to a hushed silence. A glass fell to the floor from someone's hand with a crash...

" We don't talk about that round these parts" said the Barman " best you don't mention anymore about it".

"Oh Crag you fool, you've done it again "said Esmee.

Outside the wind rose to a demonic howl, shaking the windows..

"So what'll you strangers be wanting around here" said one of the burly fisherman as he strolled over to the group's table.

'Terribly sorry old man" drawled Omah, we're here on a Research Trip funded by the government and we'll be performing some Marine Survey work off the Isle of Thought at the Trench of Thought.

"You don't look like Marine Scientists, more like a fancy dress party" said the burly fisherman.

'It was SUCH short notice' fluttered Esmee, ' no time to change I'm afraid'.

"We could use some help actually" said Sven 'we're a bit short of manpower as we had to leave in a rush'.

At this the fisherman softened. 'Aye well we don't come cheap but the fishing's piss poor so we might be able to help your little survey, I'll talk to the others When will you be setting out?'

"Tomorrow' said Sven, ' if this weather blows itself out'.

At the mention of money, the mood in the bar towards the strangers had softened. Omah started a card game with some of the locals and Big Sis challenged the burly fisherman to an arm- wrestle. She initially let him win then suggested a best of three. It had been a long time with no serious male company.

The Old Crone had disappeared earlier with the local postman who also had a pet Falcon. They were last seen walking over the heather arm in arm. Flying overhead were the Falcon and the Griffon wheeling and swooping together across the heathland looking for prey.

Chapter 75. Sabotage

Meanwhile back on the *Lagos Star,* Steward was busy below decks. He'd been locked up in one of the tool lockers since his attempt to murder Sven by throwing him overboard and was getting increasingly anxious. He realised it was only a matter of time before they reached land when he would have to face justice. Justice that would include the murder of three innocent people and an attempted murder of another. There were seven witnesses who could testify to that. He had to move fast.

After several hours with a crowbar trying to snap the door lock lever to the watertight door he managed to free himself from his temporary prison. He checked his watch- it was three a.m. The storm had blown itself out. He quietly moved through the corridors expecting to see someone but soon realised he was alone on the ship. He quickly hatched a plan of action.

He found a few emergency supplies and an inflatable safety dingy. He found ship's plans on the bridge showing where the seacock valves and their controls were located.

He would scuttle the ship, sink it by opening all the seacocks and thereby removing all evidence of the group's presence on board. He would then paddle the dingy across the bay to Barra and keep himself hidden, out of sight on the island until the next CalMac ferry arrived to Oban or Tiree. He would be just another anonymous foot passenger amongst the trucks and tourists.

The plan was set, the sabotage had begun as the *Lagos Star* started to slowly sink deeper into the waters of the bay, its rusty bulkheads creaking under this new force. In a couple of hours the water was beginning to lap the decks and it was time for the steward to launch the safety dingy and vacate..

The steward chuckled to himself as the tide carried him towards Castlebay. Looking back he could see most of the ship submerged, just some of the top superstructure still visible. He checked his progress. He would need to make land away from the harbour to avoid being seen. He was free. This was too easy!..

Chapter 76. Breakfast Shock

It was breakfast time in the Castlebay hotel. The group arranged themselves around a table and discussed the day ahead. Last nights storm had passed and the day was calm and bright. Crag had purchased a new kilt from the gift-shop and looked faintly absurd as it clashed severely with his safari jacket top. He persisted in reminding everyone that he was following Scottish tradition and was wearing no underwear but neither of the women were remotely interested, especially now they had real men to admire and banter with. The fishermen too were enjoying seeing some new women in Castlebay, especially Sis who had made such an impression with her last night's arm-wrestling.

As they were finishing breakfast, Calum The Younger from last night came into the dining room looking worried. ' Have ye no seen out in the bay today?' The group looked up. ' your ship has gone, it's disappeared!' Sven raced to the window, scanned the bay but could see nothing. He grabbed the tourist telescope from the window sill, next to where the attraction brochures were neatly stacked and he adjusted the focus. All that could be seen from where the *Lagos Star* had been anchored, was the tip of a communications mast, poking out of the water at an angle like a drunken periscope..everything else was gone.

the group was silent, shocked and bewildered ,' I suppose that's the end of the Marine Research trip' offered Calum with just a hint of sarcasm as he wandered off to tell his fishermen friends.

Sven suddenly realised..' The Steward was on board, he must have gone down with the ship!''

'What a HORRIBLE way to go' said Esmee - shuddering at the idea.'He was a killer, a murderer' said Omah' he had it coming to him, good riddance to him.'

'Shall I organise a benefit concert for him' suggested Paul, already visualising a seascape light show.

'Shut up' said Sis,'he's gone - leave it. But do we tell the Coastguard? the authorities would investigate. Do we want that?

'Our secret' said Omah ' no one needs to know. The man was evil, a killer and deserved it'.

The group sat in silence trying to absorb the enormity of events, their long journey, a failed mission and now the covering up of a drowning..'I'm having an early drink' said Sven..'anyone join me?'..

Chapter 77. Kismet

Earlier in the night, after he'd scuppered the *Lagos Star*, the Steward was rowing the inflatable dingy across the waters of Castlebay towards Barra. It was still dark but he could see the grey dawn growing from the east. The tide was with him, carrying the dingy in. He could see the small pinpricks of light from the harbour buildings slowly getting clearer. He was so excited as he revelled in his own brilliant masterplan of escape!

As he rowed on he considered where he would go next, back to Marseille perhaps? Some Mediterranean sun after the cold misery of the North Atlantic. Latch on to a rich widow and arrange an accident perhaps?

With his mind full of exciting new possibilities he wasn't aware of the subtle changes that were happening with the moving seawater under his inflatable. The short stubby paddle was making his arms ache and he didn't seem to be any nearer the shore. He began to paddle harder which made his arms hurt more but was no nearer land, in fact the outline of Castlebay seemed to receding. With a sudden sickening realisation he was aware he was drifting back out. The tide had turned and he was riding a rip tide out to sea. The Steward panicked and thrashed about with the paddle but the inflatable was not going to change direction. He started to sob as the dingy sped up and started to spin as they passed a neighbouring rocky outcrop and out into open sea. He rowed like a man possessed, cursing the sea, the sky, all of humanity until his hands were bleeding and raw with the salt. Exhausted and defeated he fell asleep.

When he woke up it was night. In his mind a few seconds of bliss, before the rocking motion forced him to remember where he was and what had happened.

All around him was blackness, the sea and the sky. It was a clear night, he could see the stars, some so bright, maybe they were planets.. The bright moon shone a greasy yellow film over the water. A few inches from him the sea around the dingy lapped with an occasional splash over the side, making the bottom increasingly sloppy. He wondered if the inflatable had a leak.

Sometime during the long night - he had no idea when - the ocean seemed to come alive, inviting him to join, to glide effortlessly into its depths. He heard the snort and blow as a whale came nearby to investigate, the click and chatter of Porpoises or was it Dolphins? Looking into the depths he saw the beautiful luminosity coming from myriads of tiny unknown sea creatures. He started to cry again, he was the stranger that didn't belong, lost in a different world. Eventually he cried himself back to sleep.

He woke with a bump. The inflatable had hit something. He looked around in the early morning light to see he was next to a ruined stone jetty. Another bump as the dingy grazed the stonework but this time accompanied by a pop and then a hiss. A jagged piece of old ironwork had punctured the dingy which was starting to deflate and sink.

The Steward grabbed the meagre supplies and threw them up onto the jetty and then tried to scramble up to the top of the seaweed covered side. His hands, already cut and blistered opened up and started bleeding again. He struggled up to the level just in time to look down and see the dingy totally deflated and drift away. A useless piece of semi submerged plastic sheet, his last chance of escape.

The dingy had delivered him to the Isle of Thought. He didn't know that but he would find out in time. He clambered up the rocks away from the water and looked around. The island was just a giant rock fortress in the ocean. In every direction he saw towering near vertical - black granite rock faces occupied by sea birds: gulls, gannets and guillemots screeching their resentment at his presence on the island. It started to rain - hard..It felt as if the whole island resented his presence.

He stumbled up some rough hewn steps and found the remnants of civilisation, some stone foundations which could once have been small rooms or cells. There were some scratched dates in the stonework - 'AD1367 In Excelsis Deo' and then another -'AD1789 Hamish McKnuckie' and that was it. No more dates or inscriptions, no sign of anyone since the 18th Century.

That wasn't strictly true. What Steward didn't know was that twice a year a group of Research Scientists and Ornithologists were airlifted in by helicopter to record the bird population - when the weather permitted which wasn't very often. Unfortunately for the Steward the last Researchers had just been and left two weeks ago.

As Steward finished his handful of provisions and the last of his drinking water, he was sure he could hear the sound of bagpipes over the wind and rain. Standing in the cold and wet he strained to listen. He was listening to the Bagpipes of Thought.

After just one day and night, he realised the situation was hopeless. The complete and total solitude ate into his soul, he didn't know whether he was hallucinating and was doubting his sanity. Sometimes he was sure he could hear his mother calling him in from the garden for tea. Other times he was back at school, in the noisy playground playing with the other children on the latest crazes - but he was always pulled back to hearing those hideous ghostly pipes.

He stood on the edge of the cliff sixty feet up from the heaving swell, watched the surf boiling as it crashed against the rocks below. He contemplated if and when he should jump - whether he would die quickly or would he lie amongst the rocks and seaweed racked with broken bones for days - only just alive? Perhaps even a slow lingering death would be preferable to the complete insanity and the constant hunger, the cold and the wet... Steward took a step forward...

Chapter 78. Exposed

Meanwhile the morning after the sinking, Sven, Crag and Omah set off in
Calum's fishing boat out into the bay where the *Lagos Star* lay submerged.
The mood was one of a funeral cortege - an irony not lost on Sven. They
were heading out to look at a watery grave in more ways than one.
They needed to moor a Marker Buoy over the sunken site for other
shipping. Calum was whistling quietly to himself - he'd seen many boats
founder and other disasters at sea, for him this was just another one.
However he was increasing suspicious of the behaviour and body-
language of his passengers. They were a weird bunch alright but there was
something more.
'What'll happen to the wreck' Sven asked to Calum.
'Och I expect they'll leave it here, perhaps leave it as a marine reef for the
fishes. No use to us fishermen though, just be in the way of the clam
dredgers. These days its all about the ecology. Us fishing folk we don't
matter'.
' How about a salvage lift operation? asked Sven. 'Any possibility?'
' Unlikely' said Calum ' the operation would cost more than the value of
the ship - unless there was a high value in one of the containers'.
'Like gold you mean' blurted Crag.
"Shut up you FOOL ' hissed Omah but too late. Calum immediately picked
up on the scent.
' I knew there was something going on with you lot! You're no more
Marine Biologists than I'm the Prince of Wales.. why are you here with
that broken down ship? Marine Research, my arse..No don't tell me, you're
the latest in a long line of gold hunters yes?..'

The game was up. It was time to come clean and tell. Calum could make
life very difficult if the authorities were called in.
'Well um yes' said Sven,' the plan was to get to the WWII sub by the
Trench of Thought - half raise it and check the cargo for the missing gold.
We hadn't counted on the North Atlantic weather. That's how we ended up
in Castlebay'. What did you mean by "a long line of gold hunters?".
"You're not the first bunch of idiots who believed the story' said Calum '
we had a Argentinian recovery team from Bueno Aires - very nasty guys,
guns and everything, that was in 1986. Then there was an American team

arrived 1998. They had the best of everything, the best ship and kit money could buy. Aye they failed too.'

'But why?' asked Omah ' the sub was there, it was seen with sonar on the ocean floor, so why?'

'The Trench' said Calum, 'the Trench of Thought is unstable. It's on the edge of a much deeper chasm.There was an undersea tremor, an eruption shift. The shelf of the Trench gave way and collapsed into the abyss taking the sub with it. There's some deep water out there, deeper than the grave of the Titanic. Whatever that sub was, Allied or German - and whatever was in it we will never know. You should have checked the Trinity House database. It has data on all recorded undersea seismic changes.'

' But how come the story is still discussed?' asked Sven.

' Have you lot never heard of the Loch Ness monster?.. Aye Nessie keeps a few hotels open there. Our Nazi gold legend makes the boat trips a bit more exciting for the summer tourists here.' With that Calum gave them a wink and started to prepare the Marker Buoy.

The fishing boat soon arrived at where the *Lagos Star* had foundered. Calum expertly manoeuvred the boat to where the communications mast was still visible and launched the buoy, lashing it to the mast and setting the flashing red beacon. He set the onboard GPS signal, leaned back, admired his work and strolled to the wheelhouse for the return journey. The return mood was subdued with no words exchanged, the only sound the throb of the diesel and the occasional scream from a gull upset that no fish scraps were being thrown overboard.

They had revealed more than they had wanted to. They felt humiliated and stupid about the failed mission. As Sven weighed up his future he was fairly sure there would be no further investigation.The mystery disappearance of the Steward would never be discussed. It was something they would have to live with.

As Calum steered the boat up to the Castlebay mooring, each of the men were privately wondering who should tell the girls the bad news. Neither Sven or Omah wanted to be the luckless messenger. As if of the same mind, Sven and Omah turned their eyes to Crag who was busy checking his trouser creases.

'Crag old man' said Omah ' You're a good chap to have in an emergency situation'

Crag couldn't help but acknowledge the fact and smiled modestly.

'You blew open the gold story and in doing so we found out the truth' said Sven, ' so it's only right you should take the credit and tell the girls. You'll be a hero in their eyes!'
Crag was already planning which of his Man on Safari outfits would best suit his new role as Senior Marine Plot Investigator and how a paisley cravat would be most appropriate. The trouser creases badly needed a press and he would also need to trim his moustache....Recognition at last!..

Written by Rick Weeks from an idea by Rick Weeks and LJ Tomlinson.

Many thanks to Alexander Kliem of Kliempictures and Engin Akyurt for allowing me to use their splendid photographic artwork on Pixabay.

Printed in Poland
by Amazon Fulfillment
Poland Sp. z o.o., Wrocław

60418666R00052